BLOOD DEBT

Other books by S.J. Stewart:

Beyond the Verde River
Outlaw's Quarry
Shadow of the Gallows

BLOOD DEBT

•

S.J. Stewart

AVALON BOOKS
NEW YORK

Published by Thomas Bouregy & Co., Inc.
160 Madison Avenue, New York, NY 10016

Library of Congress Cataloging-in-Publication Data

   Stewart, S. J.
    Blood debt / S. J. Stewart.
     p. cm.
    ISBN 0-8034-9760-1 (acid-free paper)
    1. New Mexico—Fiction. I. Title.

    PS3569.T473B58 2006
    813'.54—dc22

                  2005028543

PRINTED IN THE UNITED STATES OF AMERICA
ON ACID-FREE PAPER
BY HADDON CRAFTSMEN, BLOOMSBURG, PENNSYLVANIA

To my daughters-in-law,
Jane and Marty,
and to my cousin, Virginia.

Chapter One

Shad Wakefield was bone weary, far from home, and in no mood for human companionship when he topped a rise and spotted the campfire. He counted four men in the waning light, and was about to veer off and avoid them when he caught the aroma of coffee drifting on the wind. No doubt about it, man was subject to temptation. *Maybe those men down there have crossed paths with Toby Granger*, he told himself. Besides, they'd likely spotted him, and riding off in another direction might be looked on as unfriendly. He prodded the dun in the sides and headed toward the coffee pot. When he got closer, however, he began to doubt his judgment. One look told him that these were rough *hombres*. They were armed to the teeth. But it was too late for him to fold. He'd already tossed in his chips and there was nothing to do but play the hand. The weight of the pistol at his side was reassuring.

"Howdy," he called. "Saw your fire and smelled the coffee."

1

The one with a red beard muttered a curse and got to his feet. His face was sinewy, as if it had been cured by the sun, and his lips were so thin that his mouth appeared to be nothing more than a slit. He wore the tied-down holster of a gunslinger. It held a pearl-handled Smith and Wesson. He left no doubt that he resented Shad's intrusion and was itching for a fight. Shad watched them all carefully, especially Red. Two of them stayed put. They seemed to be waiting to see what happened. The other, who was taller and heavier and looked like he might have been a prize fighter, signaled Red to hold off. He struggled to his feet and grinned, revealing gaps in his teeth. He was wearing part of a Confederate uniform even though the war had been over for five years.

"Come on in," he invited. "I think we can spare a cup of coffee for a stranger."

They watched Shad's every move, eyes hard with suspicion. It appeared that he'd stumbled into a den of rattlesnakes. With an easy motion, he swung his leg over the saddle and dismounted. Careful not to turn his back on them, he filled a cup and held it in his left hand, leaving his gun hand free. It was an action that didn't go unnoticed.

"Where is it you're headed?" asked Gap Tooth in an off-hand way.

"South. I'm looking for a kid. He's about sixteen. Straw-colored hair and sunburnt nose. Got lots of freckles. I've been sent to fetch him home 'cause his pa is dying."

"Too bad."

"Haven't seen him, have you?"

The men exchanged glances.

"Nope," said GapTooth. "Haven't seen no kids betwixt here and Taos."

The others nodded their silent agreement.

On the western horizon, the setting sun was poised above the mountain peaks. Before long, it would be dark. He glanced over to where they'd tethered their horses and nearly scalded himself with the coffee. Among them was an Appaloosa with a banjo marking on its haunch. It was Toby Granger's horse. The stocky, mean-looking galoot with a pockmarked face noticed his interest.

"You looking to buy a fresh mount?" he asked.

Shad hid his anger. "Nope. Just want to finish my coffee and move on."

Too late. They were suspicious.

"Kind of chancy for a man to be riding out here all by his lonesome," said Gap Tooth, an underlying menace in his voice. "No telling what kind of trouble he could run into."

"I'm not exactly alone," Shad lied. "Some important folks back in Trinidad want the boy real bad. I'm only one of half a dozen that've been sent out to find him. We're to meet up shortly."

He wasn't sure his story was believed, but at least it was enough to trouble them. Maybe enough to keep them from killing him.

"What's so all-fired important about a snot-nose kid?" asked Red. "If he'd cared anything about his old man, he'd've stayed close to home."

"Maybe," said Shad. "Maybe not."

He finished his coffee with a gulp and set the cup aside. Still keeping an eye on them, he went over and mounted the dun. "Obliged for the hospitality," he said, backing away.

The sun was behind the mountains now, leaving an afterglow to see by. He could feel their hostility as they stood watching. When he'd put some distance between himself and the camp, he wheeled and galloped away. A dip in the landscape took him out of their sight.

His brow was wet with sweat in spite of the fact that the evening was cool. No doubt about it, he'd had a close call. But it didn't look like Toby had been as lucky. He had to face it. Chances were, he wouldn't be bringing the boy home. The Appaloosa with the distinctive marking was Banjo, a gift from Toby's pa in happier times. Nothing short of force would have separated the two of them.

Three months had passed since Toby Granger had packed his saddlebags and left the M Bar W, the ranch that Shad had inherited from his father. At least he'd inherited half of it. The young hothead had a temper. It didn't help that Toby's pa, Nat, was bullheaded too. During their last argument, father and son had almost come to blows. Though he'd hidden his illness, Nat had been a sick man at the time. After his son's stormy departure, his health had steadily worsened. When he begged Shad to go find his son and bring him home, Shad couldn't turn him down. Nat was more than a hired hand on his ranch. He was a friend who'd once saved Shad's life, and a man couldn't refuse such a friend his dying request.

Now he had to discover Toby's fate, even though it meant going back to that camp. He reined up and waited for darkness to deepen before he set out. The night air was cool, chilling him, now, in spite of the duster he wore. Overhead, the moon in its first quarter shed scant light on the arid landscape.

Near the camp, he dismounted and went the rest of the way on foot. Since his eyes had adjusted to the dark, he was able to spot the guard they'd posted. He was a considerable distance from the dying embers of the campfire. What was more, he'd abandoned his duty in favor of sleep. Silent as a wraith, Shad made his way over to where Banjo was picketed.

"Steady, boy," he whispered, using his knife to free the animal. Banjo recognized him as an old friend and nuzzled his collar. Shad slipped a halter around the horse's neck and led him back to the dun.

Next, he returned for the sleeping sentry. He slipped up behind him, careful to make no sound that would give him away. In a swift, sure move he disarmed the outlaw without waking him and stuffed the man's revolver in his belt. Then he covered the man's mouth and pressed a blade against his throat, shocking him to wakefulness. For what he'd likely done to Toby, Shad felt no inclination to be gentle. He forced the outlaw to his feet and walked him to where the horses waited.

"Make a sound and you're dead," he whispered.

He took the knife away in order to tie the man's hands and gag him. The outlaw tensed, as if about to call out. Instantly the knife was back in place.

"So help me, I'll kill you if you make a sound."

This time, the threat worked. He used a bandana for a gag and a piggin' string to bind his wrists. With one big heave, he hoisted the man over Banjo's back like a big sack of potatoes. Then he mounted up and headed south. When he was far enough away from the camp so that sound wouldn't carry, he hauled the prisoner down and removed the gag. It was then he got his first good look. It was Red that he'd captured, and he was mad.

While the prisoner uttered a string of curses, Shad kept his gun pointed straight at Red's belly.

"Mohler's going to shoot you for this," the outlaw threatened.

"Well, I guess he can try, but he's not here. You are. Now, if you want to live to see another sunrise, you're going to tell me what happened to Toby Granger."

"We done told you we don't know nothin' about no kid."

Shad grabbed him by the shirt front and pulled him close. "Then explain to me how you got his horse?"

"You mean that horse?" he said, nodding toward Banjo.

"Yes, that horse. What did you do with the boy who owns him?"

"Didn't do nothin'. Norm went and bought him off a miner from one of them gold camps up in the mountains."

"Norm?"

"Norm Quillen. You met him back there. One that looks like his nose got stepped on by a mule."

"What was the name of the miner? Surely you got a bill of sale." His grip tightened on the outlaw.

"Stovall. His name was Stovall. That's all I know."

"I expect you can tell me the name of the gold camp."

"It's not exactly a camp," Red amended. "He works on his own. Does some placer mining at a claim on past the Maxwell Grant. It's up on the mountain somewhere. Ask around Cimarron. They might know of him."

It wasn't much. Still, it was a start. Shad released the outlaw suddenly, causing him to stumble backward and fall. While Red was down, he loosened the outlaw's bonds with a quick knife slash.

"I'm keeping your gun. If I find that boy is dead and you've had any part in it, I intend to see that you hang."

"That mean you're letting me go?"

"For now. Go on back to camp."

"Now just a minute, I ain't walkin'. I'm riding that Appaloosa. And besides, I won that pearl-handled Smith and Wesson in a poker game back east at Fort Smith. It's worth a whole lot of money. Give it back!"

Shad thumbed the hammer on his .44 Army Remington.

"I'm not handing you a gun to shoot me with, and you're not riding that horse. I'll be keeping him until I find his owner. Or until I find out what happened to him."

"You can't expect me to go 'shank's mare'!"

"Why not? A walk in the night air will be good for you. Clear your head a little. Give you a chance to think up a reason why you were sleeping on guard duty."

Red muttered something unintelligible.

"If I were you, I'd get going. A fellow might change his mind and decide you're worth the lead it'd take to shoot you, after all."

"Just you wait," Red threatened before taking off on foot.

"Come on, Banjo," said Shad from the back of the dun. "We've got some distance to cover. I expect that pack of coyotes will be hot on our trail come sunup."

He angled to the southwest, the general direction of Cimarron. Too many hours on the trail had made him weary. He longed for the comfort of a real bed. Youth didn't help much, either, for he felt more like fifty-three than the twenty-three that he was. But there would be no rest until he'd put some distance between himself and the outlaws. He was practically asleep in the saddle when the position of the Big Dipper showed that it was only a few hours until dawn. He stopped and made camp in a wash. There he built a small fire and cooked a simple meal. The bacon and fry bread was the first food he'd eaten since early morning. He wolfed it down like a starving man. When the flames of the campfire died to nothing more than glowing embers, he moved a little distance away. He made his bed among tall clumps of rabbitbush, trusting the horses to warn him if anyone approached.

Overhead, the sky was lit with stars that were brighter than they'd ever been in Missouri, where he'd spent so many years. But St. Louis had other lights that competed. It also had smokestacks. Then, too, the air had lacked the lightness of that in Western lands.

He recalled those days in the city with a mixture of pain and pleasure. During that time, he'd read for the law, fallen in love, and lost her forever when her family abruptly moved to Ohio and married her off to a politician. Working in the West had healed most of his grief, but the memory of Letitia would always be with him. Still, he was aware that if things had gone a different way, he'd be practicing law in a dark stuffy office, while equally stuffy social events filled his spare time. For sure, he was meant to be a rancher, not a big city lawyer. On that thought, he slept.

It was shortly after dawn when he awoke. A light breeze brought with it the scent of sage. He filled his lungs. It was his best guess that the town of Cimarron was still a couple days' ride. Once he got there he'd ask around about Toby. For sure, he'd try to find the where-abouts of that gold prospector named Stovall.

When he was getting ready to pull out, Banjo came over and nuzzled him.

"Up to your old tricks, I see," he said, rubbing the horse's back. "Always wanting a treat. Afraid it's going to have to wait awhile, buddy. We've got to find that trouble-making owner of yours."

Stories of gold finds in New Mexico had enthralled young Toby. Now that he was a sixteen-year-old run-away, the gold camps would be a magnet.

Nat had tried to keep his son tied to the ranch. Tried to make a cowhand out of him. But his efforts only made things worse between them. Now, Nat was strug-gling against a disease that was sure to win. His deteri-oration was a sorry thing to watch. Doc Fairchild had told Shad and Judge Madison, who was his partner in the M Bar W, that he didn't think his patient would see another winter. This was September.

"Shad, go find my son and bring him back," Nat had pleaded. "I gotta make things right with him before it's too late."

It was a tall order. He'd wanted to say, "I can't. I don't even know where to begin." But the look in a dying man's eyes put an end to excuses before they were spoken.

On the second night after reclaiming Banjo, he camped on the lee side of a rise. All that day he'd been careful to check his back trail. Still, he'd seen no sign of the outlaws. The one called Mohler appeared to be the leader of the pack. Of course it might be that he had something more urgent to do than chase after Shad. But if Red had been calling the shots, he knew it'd be different. No doubt about it. Red had suffered humiliation and he was clearly not the type of man to forget.

He was drifting off to sleep when he heard a soft rustling noise in the brush. Instantly alert, his hand grasped the butt of his revolver. Whoever was out there wasn't taking any chances. He continued to feign sleep.

"Oh, I know you're awake," said a familiar voice from the shadows. "If you're fixin' to shoot, I'd appreciate it if you'd hold off."

"Abe Featherstone! What in blazes are you doing way down here? You scared the dickens out of me."

His old friend came forward, leading a couple of horses. "Glad you're so happy to see me," he said sarcastically.

"I wasn't expecting you. Thought you might be someone with malicious intent."

Abe chuckled. "Still throwing around them big words you learned at that Eastern school, I see. Truth to tell, His Honor sent me. He figured you could use some help and, as usual, he was right."

His Honor was Judge Harley Madison, who was more than a partner in a large ranching operation. He'd been Shad's guardian after his father's murder years earlier.

"What do you mean about the Judge being right?" he asked.

"I haven't been trailing too far behind you. Yesterday, I happened across the path of four owlhoots who want to get their hands on you real bad."

"I expect so. They're the ones who stole Banjo. I took him away from them."

"They had Banjo?"

"Yes, I know. It doesn't look good for Toby."

"He's not the only one. I was suspicious when I spotted 'em. Hard not to be. When they stopped for the night, I circled around and got ahead of 'em. Then turned back like I was going north. When I came up to 'em, the one with the red beard gave me your description like he'd memorized it. Asked if I'd passed you on the trail. Said you was a friend of theirs, and that they owed you a debt they wanted to repay."

Shad squatted on his haunches and added bits and pieces of dried grass to the coals.

"Afraid it's not money they want to repay. Aside from rescuing Banjo, I got a little rough with Red so he'd tell me what they'd done with Toby."

"Did he tell you?"

"No. Claimed they bought the Appaloosa from a gold prospector named Stovall. Anyway, I'm headed for Cimarron. Maybe somebody in town has seen the boy or can tell me how to find this Stovall."

"Well, if you want my opinion, we'd better get an early start. I rode hard to get here ahead of 'em. They're not too far behind."

The fire blazed back to life and Shad put the coffee pot on.

"I'll have to face them sooner or later," he said. "But I prefer later. I promised Nat I'd find Toby. I only hope that he's still alive."

"Well, I'm here to cover your back and do whatever else is needed."

Abe, lean and weathered with streaks of gray in his dark hair, was the most dependable man he knew. A friend of Shad's lawman father before Shad was born, he knew how to handle a gun.

"Look, Abe," he said, "you don't have to get mixed

up in this business. You know there's not another man I'd rather have at my side, but I think you should get away from here while you can."

Abe clamped a hand on his shoulder. "Look, I'm not ridin' out on you, Shadrach. This is my business too. Nat's been a mighty good friend. Besides, the Judge would skin me alive if I abandoned you. You're a son to him. Wouldn't feel none too good about it, myself."

"Then we'd better drink our coffee, try to get a few hours' sleep, and move on at first light."

In the gray mist that preceded sunrise, they packed their gear and headed for the trail town of Cimarron. On its outskirts, they reined up and looked it over. It was a bustling community, larger than he'd expected.

"The place sure looks bigger than the last time I was here," said Abe. "It just keeps on growing."

"Well, let's ride on in and see what we can find out."

"This Stovall fellow that you mentioned," said Abe, "do you suppose he's mixed up with them outlaws?"

"Don't ask me. But whether he is or not, I'd sure like to hear what he's got to say about Toby."

Saddle leather squeaked as Abe shifted his weight. "What're the chances of his being here in Cimarron, do you reckon?"

"Slim to none. But somebody around here ought to know where to find him."

The town had long been a stop on the Santa Fe Trail. It could brag of a grist mill, a fine-looking hotel, saloons, and a bunch of other businesses. It had a wide, dusty street that was lined with buildings.

"How about we try that saloon over there?" said Abe. "Best place I know to find out something."

The establishment was fancier than Shad had

expected. It sported a mahogany bar with a big brass-rimmed mirror behind it. Over the player-piano hung a picture of a buxom lady who bore a strong resemblance to a society matron he'd known back in St. Louis. Near the door stood a shiny spittoon. The center of the room was filled with tables and chairs. Another few hours and the place would likely be full. But since it was late afternoon, it was almost empty. The paunchy, round-faced barkeep looked up when they entered.

"What'll you gents have?" he asked.

"Whiskey," said Abe, placing a gold coin on the counter top. "Make that two, with a little information to go along with the drinks."

The barkeep eyed the coin and set out two glasses, which he filled with a bottle from his stock.

"Exactly what is it you want to know?"

"Have you heard of a fellow named Stovall? If so, where can we find him?"

He looked sharply at Abe. "What is it you want with old Davie?"

"I figure that's our business," said Abe.

The barkeep hesitated, but gold has powers of persuasion. "Well, he comes in here sometimes, but I understand he's working a claim on the other side of Baldy Mountain. Don't know exactly where."

"Ever figure him to be mixed up with outlaws?"

The man looked surprised. "Old Davie? Naw, not him. All he's interested in is his gold claim and his mules."

Shad wanted to find out what he knew about the outlaws.

"You ever hear of a gang that's led by a man named Mohler?"

The question clearly startled the barkeep. He glanced at the corner where his two other customers were seated. Then, leaning forward, he spoke in a conspiratorial voice that Shad could barely hear.

"Mohler is a bad one and he's got friends hereabouts. So's Red Thurman who rides with him. Heard that Norm Quillen and Artie Strong are with him, too. You'd better steer clear of that bunch, mister. Why, Mohler's even been seen in the company of Clay Allison. Seen them myself in this very saloon."

He'd heard of Allison. A cold-blooded killer by reputation. He was known to be especially dangerous when he was drunk.

"What about a boy with straw-colored hair? Big for his age, which happens to be sixteen. Usually has a lopsided grin and a sunburnt nose. You seen him?"

He shook his head. "No, he didn't come in here. That's not to say he wasn't in town, though."

Abe shoved the coin toward the barkeep. "Obliged for the information."

Once they were outside, he asked Shad what he thought.

"Until we find Toby, we're going to have to keep a step ahead of Mohler and his outfit. Right now that miner, Stovall, is the best lead we've got. I reckon we'd better head for that mountain."

First, they took time to stop at the livery stable and feed the horses. Abe was riding a big gray gelding and leading a pretty black with a white blaze. Shad had his own horse, Squire, and he had Toby's Appaloosa to care for. When, at last, they rode out of Cimarron, he had the strange feeling that he was escaping—and just in the nick of time.

Chapter Two

Shad admitted to himself that he was pleased his old friend had tagged along. Abe was a good man to have around in times of trouble, and this was decidedly a troubled time. Far to the west, a range of mountain peaks rose up, seeming to touch the sky. Toward the east, the high plains stretched to the horizon, where they disappeared around the curve of the earth. In the mountains they would seek Davie Stovall.

Although some called this part of New Mexico a desert, it didn't seem so to him. A vast carpet of rabbitbush had yellowed up, turning the landscape a brilliant gold. *Chamisa* the Mexican folks called it. Beyond were the spiky yucca plants that had so many practical uses, like easing pain and washing hair.

"*Chamisa* gold is a whole lot prettier than the stuff that's panned from streams and dug from quartz," said Abe, sensing his thoughts. "For my part, I wouldn't want to be rich. Not that kind of rich, anyway. Too dangerous."

15

"You mean somebody's always going to try to take it away from you?"

"That too. But I was thinking about something else. You see, sometimes when a man gets a lot of money, all of a sudden it's not enough. He keeps wanting more and more. After a while, there comes a time when he stops caring about how he gets it. Money can get a hold on a fellow. Change him from what he was. Now, I don't have much, but I'm satisfied with what I've got."

Shad mulled this over for a time. "Well, my friend," he said, "I expect when a man's satisfied with his life, he's got a bigger treasure than the kind they lock up in bank vaults."

"Kind of how I read it. Fact is, you can bet your saddle on it. A man who's got a warm bed, plenty to eat, and good friends hasn't got nothin' to complain about."

Shad didn't say it, but he could think of a few things to complain about. Like aching muscles and the pressure of keeping ahead of a gang of outlaws. Added to that was the aggravation of tracking down a runaway kid who didn't want to be found—or who might be dead.

At dusk they stopped. Much as Shad wanted to put more distance between himself and Cimarron, they needed to rest the horses and wait for daylight. Besides, he could use some rest, himself. They moved off the trail a ways to make camp in the brush. It was a safer place in case the outlaws closed in. He was counting on the lure of the saloon and its stock of whiskey to keep Mohler and his bunch in town for a while, but nothing was a sure thing except death and trouble.

They spread their bedrolls behind some rabbitbush

and ate a cold supper before crawling into their blankets. In the quiet of the night, worrying thoughts intruded.

"Abe," Shad said, "you've seen Nat. How much longer do you think he can last?"

He heard the older man turning, trying for a more comfortable position. "You afraid you're down here on a fool's errand?"

Truth was, that was exactly what he was thinking. "Maybe something like that," he admitted.

"Well, don't you believe it. Not for a minute. When a man wants to hang on as bad as Nat does, he's going to hang on. The rest of it is up to us. We've got to find his runaway boy and bring him home, one way or another."

Easy to say. A whole lot harder to do. That night his sleep was fitful and wracked with nightmares.

Shortly before daylight, Abe shook him awake. "Son, I think you'd sleep all day if it wasn't for me," he joked. "We'd better get a move on. The closer to the canyon we get, the better I'll feel."

They skipped breakfast and saddled up. The pre-dawn cold penetrated Shad's clothes and wrapped around his bones. His stomach complained of being empty, and he longed for a cup of hot coffee to thaw his insides.

"How far is it to the Cimarron Canyon?" he asked.

"I've only been down here twice, but I'm guessing we're maybe six or seven miles out. Not any more than that, I reckon."

The sun had climbed higher and was warming Shad's back when they spotted the stranded freight wagon.

"Looks like somebody's got trouble," said Abe.

The driver jumped down and waved his arms to attract their attention. Wasted energy. Nobody could help but see him and his predicament.

"Howdy," said Abe as they rode up.

"And howdy back to you. How about helping me out here? Hit a rock and the wheel came off." The driver's voice was raspy, like he needed to swallow a bottle of oil to lubricate his throat. He was slight of build and there was no way he could have put that wheel back on by himself.

"Be glad to," said Shad, silently begrudging the delay this would cause.

They looked around and found a sturdy dead-fall tree limb to use as a lever. While he and Abe hoisted the corner of the wagon, the driver slipped the wheel back on. It was plenty warm now, and he wiped a sleeve across his sweaty face.

"Look, I want to thank you fellows for your help," said the freighter. "Don't know what I'd have done if you hadn't come along. Name's Russ Lassen."

Shad told him their names. "Glad to help," he said, "but we've got to be moving on. You'd best keep watch for a bunch of outlaws that are sure to be following us. There's four of 'em. If you've got a gun, best to keep it handy."

A look of fear crossed the freighter's clean-shaven face. "Say, we're all going in the same direction. Why don't we stick together for a while?"

Shad and Abe exchanged glances. The lumbering freight wagon would slow them down. But, after all, it was their fault that its driver and cargo had been placed in danger.

"All right," Shad said. "But we're searching for a kid in order to bring him home before his pa dies."

"What's that got to do with outlaws?" asked Lassen, looking puzzled.

A fair question. "I found this Appaloosa in amongst their horses. It belongs to the boy. I took it back and tried to make one of 'em tell me how he'd come by it. He claimed he got it from a miner named Stovall. The barkeep at Cimarron was acquainted with Stovall and told me where he was working."

When Stovall's name was mentioned, Lassen looked surprised.

"I don't know how Davie is mixed up in all of this, but I can assure you that he wouldn't hurt a fly."

"Do you know him?"

"Sure. He's working a claim over near Last Chance. By the way, what does this kid you're after look alike?"

When Shad gave him Toby's description, he was rewarded with another look of surprise.

"I think I've seen him. At least I saw a kid who fits that description."

"Where?" he asked.

"Awhile back, I was intercepted by a hermit who holes up in the mountains. Big hairy fellow. Lots of gray in his beard. Some of the men have taken to calling him the Mad Hatter after the character in that *Alice* book. Well, one day he just pops out on the trail in front of me and asks what I've got in the wagon. I tell him, 'I'm hauling supplies to the gold camps.' Well, he wanted flour, cornmeal, tea, and some other stuff. So I unload what he orders, hoping to get rid of him without getting shot, and this fellow who doesn't look like he's got two coins to rub together pays me in cash. Thing of it is, all the time this transaction is going on, there's a kid standing back at the edge of the trees. He fits the description of this runaway you're hunting for right down to the freckles."

Shad felt a surge of hope. "Do you know where this Mad Hatter has his place?"

Lassen shook his head. "Nobody knows that. Best I can do is show you where he waylaid my wagon."

"Then let's get on with it," said Abe. "We're standing here burning daylight."

They escorted Lassen and his cargo into the canyon, where pines and oak trees hugged the trail and forested the flanks. Beside them the sprightly Cimarron River tumbled onward toward the plains. It had carved a deep impressive cut in the land, yet in most places it was narrow enough for a man to jump across. All the while, Shad was thinking about Lassen. The voice was wrong. The hands too small. The face too smooth.

After a time, Abe signaled him to fall back.

"What's up?" he asked.

"Wanted to have a word with you, that's all." There was an odd look on his face.

"Well?"

"Our friend Lassen is no man."

"Yeah. I'd pretty much figured that out. What I'd like to know is why a woman is disguised as a man and hauling freight around the country all by herself."

"You ought to ask her about that."

"You ask her."

"Might just do that whenever the time is right."

The right time didn't come until evening. They were sitting near the campfire eating a hot meal, topped off with canned peaches from Lassen's stock. It was the first decent meal Shad had eaten in a long time. All the while, he tried to avoid looking at her. But one glance told him that the freight driver's face was free of stubble after a long day. The smooth face was soft and right next door to pretty. With the gloves off, her hands looked even smaller than before. They were almost dainty.

"You've figured it out, haven't you?" said a woman's voice, no longer raspy.

"Afraid so, ma'am," said Abe. "We thought it best, though, to mind our own business."

A white lie on Abe's part. He was every bit as curious as Shad to find out what this was all about.

"Perhaps I'd better explain. First off, my rightful name is Larkspur Russell. Lark to my friends. My father up and died of a bad heart and overwork a few years back. I'd never married and he didn't leave me much of anything. What was I to do? He had a wagon and a team of mules for hauling freight up to Elizabethtown and some of the other mining camps. It seemed perfectly natural that I take his place. But as a woman, I wouldn't have been accepted. In disguise, I can earn a good living."

"It's a hard job for a woman, ma'am." said Abe, looking at her with respect. "You seem to have done real well, though. Me and Shad promise we won't tell a soul."

"Thank you. You're both gentlemen. And please call me Lark whenever no one is around."

Shad guessed that Lark was several years older than himself, maybe thirty. He tried to imagine her in the feminine trappings that made women look nice, but it wasn't easy.

There was surprisingly little awkwardness when they bedded down for the night. Lark took a place on the far side of the wagon, near where the mules were tethered. Shad and Abe took the other side, keeping their distance both from Lark and from the fire they'd let burn low.

"We've had some luck," said Abe. "Can't expect it to last, though."

Knowing how fickle luck tended to be, it was something Shad always welcomed but never counted on. With a full belly, he was glad to drift off to sleep, leaving it to the horses to warn them if strangers approached.

He had no idea how much time had passed when his sleep was disturbed by a noise. Instantly, he was awake. His senses alert. Someone was lurking nearby. His hand went to the pistol beside him and closed on the grips. Feigning sleep, he lay there listening. The loudest noise was Abe's steady snoring. If Lark was awake, he couldn't tell, for she was too far away. The horses were restive, as if sensing an intruder. Probably it was one of them that had woken him. While he watched from half-closed eyes, a shadowy figure sneaked into camp. In the moonlight, he could see the man pause and look around to make sure he hadn't been detected. Reassured, he lit a match. Shielding its flame from the wind with one hand, he went over and looked at the contents of the wagon.

Quietly, Shad got to his feet and pointed the .44 at the intruder. "Looking for something?" he asked.

The man jumped like he'd already been shot. The match flame blew out. Still, there was enough night light to see by.

"Keep your hands up," Shad ordered. "If you make any move toward that pistol, I'll shoot you right between the eyes."

"Now, hold your fire, mister," the man said. "I didn't mean no harm."

"What did you mean, then? You sneaked into our camp and were going through the contents of the wagon."

Abe and Lark were awake and on their feet. Abe came over and stood beside him, gun in hand. Lark was half-hidden by the wagon.

"Would you be the fellow that's looking high and low for a runaway kid?" asked the stranger.

Shad's gut muscles tightened. He had a bad feeling about this man.

"I'm the one. What do you know about it?"

"Name's Hiram Scott. Schultz, the barkeep back in Cimarron, sent me. Said to tell you that Mohler's been on the rampage. Soon as him and his gang sober up enough to ride they'll be on your trail."

"What else did he say?"

"That Mohler's telling it all over Cimarron how you're a horse thief who ought to be hung from the nearest tree limb."

"He probably didn't mention how he stole that horse from a kid. All I did was take it back."

"Nope. Didn't say a word about that."

Mohler must have arrived right after they'd left town. He had to in order for Scott to know all of this. Then Scott hadn't wasted any time setting out on their trail.

"Schultz is a good man," said Lark, the rasp back in her voice.

"Most folks think so," agreed Scott. "Anyway, if I could trouble you to lower your guns and offer me some hot coffee and maybe a bite to eat, I'll be on my way."

Only the moonlight and a sprinkling of stars relieved the darkness of the high-up canyon. A fire would be seen a long way in either direction, a beacon to anyone watching for it. Abe pointed this out.

"We'd be plumb foolish to light a fire. Guess you'll have to pass on breakfast."

Scott didn't like what he was hearing. It was clear that he wanted that fire lit. "You're getting mighty skittish," he taunted. "I told you that Mohler and his gang won't be leaving town before morning."

"We heard what you told us," said Shad. "But the fact is, we don't know you from Adam's grandson."

He wasn't about to trust a man who'd sneak into camp at night and nose around in people's belongings. That wasn't the action of an honest man. Then, too, why would a barkeep go to the trouble of sending Scott all this distance to tell him what he already knew—that he was being pursued by outlaws. It was too much like a story made up on the spur of the moment after being caught. It looked like Abe wasn't warming up to him either.

"As for being skittish, it's saved my bacon on more than one occasion," he went on. "I've learned to mistrust strangers until I have a reason to change my mind."

Clearly, this wasn't going the way Scott wanted. He started edging away. "Guess I'll be heading on back if that's the way you feel about it."

"Don't be in such a big hurry," said Shad. "We're anxious to hear some more about Mohler."

Scott wasn't having any of it. "I've already said all I'm going to." His voice was ugly, all pretense of pleasantness abandoned.

"It was Mohler that sent you on ahead, wasn't it? How far back is he?"

Without answering, Scott went for his gun. In the dim light, body shapes were visible and Shad saw him start to draw. In one swift move, he grabbed for his own .44 and felt it buck when he fired. Scott's shot came an instant later and it was close. But it was the outlaw who went down. All around, the smell of sulphur filled the night air. Over by the wagon, Lark cried softly.

Abe ran up and kicked Scott's gun away. "If the outlaws are anywhere close, they heard that noise. We'd better haul ourselves out of here pronto."

Shad knelt to make certain the man who called himself Scott was dead. He was.

"Abe, pack our stuff. I'll get Lark's lantern and help her hitch up the team."

When they were ready to go, they dragged Scott's body into the woods. Wasting no time, they covered him with dirt using shovels from Lark's supplies. By the time the job was done, pink tendrils of dawn were showing in the eastern sky. Within a few minutes, they were heading out.

"That old boy didn't have you fooled for a minute, did he?" said Abe.

"Not the way he sneaked in there."

"Another member of the gang, no doubt. One that wasn't around when you happened on to 'em. He wasn't with 'em when I spotted 'em, either. They probably met up with him again in Cimarron."

Shad admitted to himself that he'd been careless. He

couldn't afford to be careless again. His empty stomach would be a reminder, for there would be no breakfast again this morning.

The sun's appearance was welcomed with birdsong. Winged creatures had none of the concerns of man and were content to fly about, fill their bellies, and make noises. So far, there was no sign of Mohler. Nor of the rest of his gang.

"I think we got lucky again," said Abe. "But I guess we'll know for sure if we're able to get out of this canyon without gettin' shot."

Chapter Three

It was getting close to midday when they dropped out of the canyon and entered the wide valley that stretched to the base of the mountains. Here the going was easier. The big drawback was lack of cover.

"Taos is on the other side of the *Sangre de Cristos,*" said Abe, pointing to the mountain range ahead. "Old Kit lived in Taos with his wife and kids. Had him a sizeable house there on the plaza. They say it was him that scouted the trail betwixt there and Cimarron."

Shad didn't doubt it. Carson was a legend.

"We're going to turn and go north, though," said Lark. "I think the hermit's hideout must be somewhere close to the place where he stopped me."

Shad figured she was right. A smart man wouldn't want to carry his supplies any farther than he had to.

He'd been thinking about Scott and why he'd been sent to their camp alone. Since he'd tried to get them to start a fire, it was a good guess that at least one of the others had been camped in the canyon, close enough to spot the signal. The barkeep might have told Mohler about him and Abe. But the addition of Lark and the wagon would have been a surprise to his henchman. Shad's own surprise was the fact there had been no pursuit. Had the gang been close, it would have been an easy matter to catch up with the slow-moving freight wagon. Unless they were biding their time, waiting for them to reach the valley where cover was sparse. It wasn't easy to think on, but if those outlaws came riding out of the canyon, there was apt to be a bloodbath. What was more, Lark would be right in the middle of it.

"I'll feel a whole lot easier when we get across this open space," said Abe, who'd been thinking along the same lines.

Shad saw cattle grazing on the grass and noticed there was a ranch house in the distance. He figured there was probably more than one, for the valley was big.

While crossing the broad, flat expanse, he checked their back trail often. When, at last, they turned onto a trail that led north into the mountains, he felt a sense of relief. The others did, too, he suspected. A chill wind blew down from the peaks, warning that winter in the high country was lurking. There was cloud cover now, and Lark removed her hat, letting her shoulder-length hair blow free. She was past the fresh bloom of youth but nonetheless still handsome. Smart, too. Facts that Abe was noticing. At first Shad was amused at the older man's attentions to Lark. But Abe had a lot of good years left. Why shouldn't he settle down in harness with a good woman? This one seemed pretty independent, though. She might have other ideas.

Once they'd climbed out of the valley, they found themselves among towering, dense-needled firs and bright golden aspens. A tall mountain peak to the north sported a mantle of snow. They were on the new trail for more than an hour when Lark halted her team.

"Something wrong?" asked Abe, riding to her side.

"I think this is the place where the hermit stopped me. He came down from that slope and went back that way too."

Shad slid out of the saddle. Going over to the edge, he squatted on his haunches and studied the ground closely. Time had passed. Too much of it. If Lark was right, and this was the spot where she'd been waylaid, wind and rain had wiped out all traces of the Mad Hatter's trail.

"I'm going to scout around," he said. "See what I can find."

Lark watched from the wagon. "Why don't you fellows go on together? I'll be all right. If those outlaws were going to attack, it seems to me they'd have done it by now. I've got to deliver this stuff."

Abe hesitated. "Are you sure?"

"Yes," she said, patting the shotgun at her side. Then, reaching into the wagon, she drew out a small packet. "Here, take this along. It might make you more welcome if you come across our friend." She tossed him a packet of sugar.

"Obliged," said Abe. "And if you should come across that Stovall fellow, ask him what he knows about Toby."

"I'll do that. But I know Davie Stovall like the back of my hand and I'm sure he didn't hurt that boy."

Abe stood beside the gray, watching Lark drive on up the mountain trail. He had a strange look on his face. Shad was tempted to tease his friend about the lady freight hauler but decided against it. There were some things you simply didn't make light of.

"Let's get a move on," Abe said when she'd turned out of sight.

The horses cat-hopped up the slope, into the thick of the trees. Once there, they threaded their way along the most accessible route. Shad paused here and there to cut slash marks on the bark, marking the way.

"A man could get lost up here real easy," he said.

"Don't have to tell me," said Abe. "This hermit fellow must be part mountain goat."

It turned out that Lark had been right about the place she'd picked to stop, for they soon crossed a faint trail.

"What do you bet this takes us straight to the Mad Hatter?" said Shad.

"There's only one way to find out."

It twisted and turned and led them steadily upward. Shad was thankful the horses were sure-footed. Winding single-file through the aspens and the evergreens, they rode in silence. Then, without warning, they came to a break in the forest. Above them loomed a sandstone overhang.

"Can't say as I like this," said Abe. "A man could get picked off real easy from up there."

Shad didn't like it either. Still, they had to press on ahead or else turn around and go back. He recalled the pleading look on Nat Granger's haggard face when last they'd talked. There would be no turning back.

At some time in the past, erosion had done its work, causing loose rocks and boulders to spill down from above. They'd come to rest on this narrow shoulder of the mountain, scattered like a giant's marbles. Shad squinted up at the overhang. Best he could tell, there was no sign of anyone lurking there.

"Ready?" he asked his partner.

" 'Bout as ready as I'm ever goin' to be."

Warily, they picked their way across the rock-strewn terrain. Was this the Mad Hatter's front yard? Shad wondered. When they were about a dozen yards from cover, the sound of a gunshot rent the stillness of the mountain wilderness. A sniper was at the overhang. Shad kicked the dun in the sides and raced the remaining distance. He was aware that Abe was right beside him. When they reached the relative safety of the trees, they stopped and turned.

"Looks to me like we've found him," said Abe.

"I'd bet the ranch on it."

"Think we can convince him that we're harmless? That we simply want to have a few words with him?"

"Looks to me like we've got no choice but to try. Wait here."

Shad climbed down and walked over to the edge of the trees. Cupping his hands around his mouth, he shouted, "Hold your fire! We're here to talk, that's all!"

No answer. He waited a minute and tried again. Whoever was up there was hidden, and aimed to stay that way.

"Look, we're not after you!" Shad yelled. "We're trying to find someone else and we think you can give us a lead!"

"You wanna talk, then talk to my rifle!" came the reply. "You've got nothing to say to me that I want to hear."

Abe stepped up beside him. "Nothin's easy, Shadrach," he said. "You're going to have to try again. Reason with him."

"If you ask me, I don't think he knows the meaning of the word."

"Well, it's up to you."

Shad looked up at the sniper's hiding place. "You, up there! We've been told you've got a boy with you. His name is Toby Granger. His pa's dying and he sent us to fetch him home. Wants to see him again before he crosses over."

"That's a barefaced lie!" It was Toby. "You're playing a dirty trick, Shad Wakefield, to get me to come back to that run-down cow ranch. Well, I ain't buying it. There's nothing wrong with my pa except he's mean and bullheaded."

"Young whelp," said Abe. "If'n I was in Nat's place, I'd be saying, 'good riddance.'"

By this time, Shad was feeling the same way. Still, he'd made a promise to a dying friend who'd once saved his life. He intended to keep that promise.

"I'm not lying about your pa," he said. "As for keeping you on the ranch, me and Abe don't give a hoot where you go or what you do. You're not a good hand. Fact is, you're a pain in the backside. But your pa asked me to fetch you home, and I owe him. He's hanging on from day to day, trying to stay alive 'til you get there."

"Liar!" yelled Toby. "Now, get on out of here and leave me alone." A rifle shot punctuated his order.

Abe swore. "Young donkey ain't got a brain in his head. Don't know why Nat wants him back so bad."

Shad leaned against a tree and studied the situation. "We've got to get up there somehow and try to convince that fool kid we're telling the truth."

"If you think he'll listen, I'm game. But how do we do it? And what do we do about the Mad Hatter? He's got a gun and he ain't shy about using it."

Shad breathed deeply of the cool, fir-scented air.

"Tell me, Abe, why do some people cut themselves off from the rest of the world and live alone like that? I'd go crazy."

"Could be they're crazy to start with. Or maybe they like their own company a heap better than they like anybody else's."

An idea occurred to him. "What if we convinced the old man that keeping Toby would bring a whole lot of people flocking up here to his hermitage. That because of the kid he'd never get another minute's peace or privacy."

Abe chuckled. "Now, there's a thought. Put that way, I bet he'd throw that young whelp out quick enough. Might even go so far as to kick his backside down the mountain for us. But how are you going to get the message across? That appears to be a hardheaded fellow who don't like to listen."

He'd hit it right square on the peg. They had to find a way to talk to the hermit and make him listen to reason. A thought flitted across Shad's mind and a plan started to form.

"A cautious man like that would have a back way in and out of his stronghold. If we can find it, chances are he won't be watching it. He can't keep an eye on two places at once."

"What about Toby?"

"I doubt that Toby would shoot us, even if he caught us."

"Pigheaded as he is, I wouldn't want to stake my life on it."

"We'll have to risk it. Come on. It beats standing here doing nothing."

They made their way through the trees, following the

curve of the mountain as they moved away from the overhang.

A red-tailed hawk circled now that the shooting had stopped. Gliding on an air current, it swooped to look them over. Curiosity satisfied, it flew off.

"There are kids that age who've got some sense," said Abe. "It's a shame that Toby Granger ain't one of 'em. But his pa sets store by him, and the poor fellow won't be around to see his boy get any older or wiser."

It was true enough, and Shad felt bad for Nat. When it was a man's time to go, what did he have to leave behind that counted for much? Mostly it was flesh and blood so he could pass down something of himself through the generations. Money and land couldn't be relied on and most men died with little or none of either. It was blood that counted. Too bad that it didn't count with Toby. Shad thought of his own father and how much he'd regretted not having the chance to say good-bye. Toby Granger was throwing that precious chance away like it was nothing.

Shad recalled that dark day when his lawman father was bushwhacked by an outlaw. Almost as bad were the pain-filled days that followed. He'd been made the ward of Judge Harley Madison and sent to live with the Judge's sister in St. Louis. There he was educated and there he studied for the law. But his roots were in the West and it had drawn him back like a magnet. It had come as a surprise to learn his father's secret. Before his death, Dunham Wakefield had gone partners with the Judge to lay claim to and stock a ranch. But Shad wasn't to be told about this until he was ready to settle down and take on the responsibility of running it. If, indeed, that was what he chose to do. His father had been a good man, and after all these years, Shad still missed him.

"Looks like night is going to catch us," said Abe.

The unfamiliar terrain was steep and hazardous. It would be courting disaster to go stumbling around in the dark.

"Better stop," said Shad. "We'll make a cold camp and go on at dawn."

They spread their bedrolls beneath the shelter of a big fir tree and chewed on the jerky that Abe had brought along in his saddlebag. When they were bedded down, Shad asked his friend about Larkspur Russell.

"What do you think of her? She's not your usual woman, is she?"

"Not by a long shot. She's got starch in her backbone. Guess she has to in her line of work. I admire her for it."

Moments of silence passed, broken only by the call of a night bird and the sigh of the wind in the firs. Moments stretched into hours.

By the time dawn broke on the east edge of the mountain, they were packed and ready to ride. The deadly overhang was far behind them. Here, they could climb without being spotted from above. Once high enough, they'd be able to circle around and approach the Mad Hatter's place from the back.

From the look on Abe's face, it was clear that he was in a grumpy mood. But then late September nights were cold at this altitude. No doubt his joints complained. Foregoing yet another breakfast wasn't going to help his disposition any, either.

"A fellow ought to get his fill of coffee and a mouthful

or two of bacon once in a while," he complained. "Meals have been few and skimpy lately."

"Have to tighten your belt and dream of Cook's flapjacks."

Ptolemy Hagen, known simply as Cook, made flapjacks that would melt in your mouth. He brewed good coffee too, and managed to make even the toughest game bird palatable. He was a genius of the cookstove. Hagen was Judge Madison's find and treasured by all the hands at the M Bar W. But Cook was miles away and they were hungry men.

They made their way through the forest, always climbing. When they were high enough, they turned back in the direction of the outcrop. It took awhile, but at last they reached the clearing behind it.

"Got him a nice place," said Abe.

He was looking at the snug cabin that was neatly hidden in the firs, a good distance back from the overhang. The trees that hugged the place would filter the chimney smoke and render it invisible. From that rock overhang at the front, the hermit could spot anyone approaching and get a good shot at them. All other approaches were difficult to impossible. Even passing across the open space and circling around as they had done was dangerous. If the old man had really wanted them dead, they'd now be buzzard bait. The hermit had chosen his hermitage well.

"How are we going to do this?" asked Abe. "That old man seems serious about running us off."

"We'll picket the horses here. You sneak around back. A man who thinks the way he does is sure to have a back door, or at least a window. While you're doing that, I'll make a frontal assault."

Abe nodded. "Just remember how to duck, *amigo.*"

"Goes without saying."

Shad gave Abe a few minutes to get into position. Then he started walking toward the front door. The .44 was strapped to his side. He was a good shot, but he hated like the dickens to think about killing either one of the two he was about to face. If he was forced to shoot Toby, his trip would be wasted, and he'd never be able to face Nat.

"Hello, the house!" he called, his heart thumping like a steam engine. There was a crash inside like somebody had jumped or fallen out of bed. Someone cracked a shutter and poked the end of a shotgun through the opening.

"What is it you want?" called an old man's voice. "Go away and leave me be."

"I want what I came for. To keep a promise to a dying friend. Let us have the boy. Just as soon as his pa is dead and buried, he can come on back here, or go straight to purgatory for all I care."

"The boy don't want to leave. He says you're lying."

Shad fought back his disgust and anger and kept his voice level.

"Neither me nor his pa cares a barrel of shucks what he wants. It's what his pa wants that counts. And for some reason that's beyond me, he wants that no-account boy of his to come home so he can see him one last time before he dies."

No response. He trusted Abe was in place, ready to rush the cabin on his signal. But before he could give it, the shutter was thrown open.

"Come on in then, if you've a mind to. Tell that feller out back to come in, as well. But if you're set on keeping your firearms, I reckon I'll keep mine handy, too."

"No, Cornelius!" Toby yelled. "Don't let 'em in."

Shad was aggravated enough to spit. Had he been so mule-headed at that age? Somehow, he didn't think so. Surely he would've remembered.

Cautiously, he walked forward. Abe came around the corner of the cabin and joined him. The door opened and a graybeard with steely blue eyes stood ready to meet them, shotgun in hand. They hesitated.

"Well, don't just stand there," the man chided. "You've traveled all this way and dodged my bullets. Come on inside."

When Shad crossed the threshold, it took a moment for his eyes to adjust to the darker interior. When they did, he spotted Toby Granger sulking in a corner.

The boy was big for his sixteen years, almost as tall and filled-out as Shad. His straw-colored hair had grown shaggy, and his straggly whiskers had been left untouched. Except for the eyes, a bright, clear blue, there was nothing at all about Toby Granger that would remind anyone of his father.

Shad's patience was worn thin. "Why did you go and sell Banjo to a bunch of outlaws?" he demanded to know.

Toby looked shocked. "How did you know about Banjo?"

"Never mind. I want to know how you could sell your father's present that way."

The kid looked shamefaced. "I didn't sell him. But it's a long story and you wouldn't believe me anyway."

The hermit, Cornelius, had evidently made up his mind about them. He went over and leaned his shotgun against the wall.

"While you fellers are palavering," he said, "I'll put

some coffee on to boil. If you're hungry, I'll stir up some flapjacks. Even got some honey to pour over 'em."

"We'd be obliged," said Abe. "It's been a long time since either of us had a decent meal."

"By the way," said Shad, remembering the packet of sugar that Lark had tossed him, "this is a gift from a friend."

"What friend?" asked Cornelius, hefting the sweetener he'd been given.

"The one who delivers supplies to the mining camps."

"Oh, yes. Met him once. Scrawny little thing, he was. Next time you see him, give him my thanks."

Abe looked amused at his description of Lark, but said nothing.

While the hermit set about his task of fixing flapjacks, Toby told them how he'd taken up with the outlaws.

"I'm a grown man. It was high time I was on my own. So I came down here to New Mexico Territory to get rich. It happened that I teamed up with a fellow named Stovall, who'd filed on a claim. We were starting to have a little luck at placer mining. Found some color in the creek. Then Red Thurman happened by. Told me I could get rich right away if I joined up with him and his friends. The way he talked, bragging like he was, I believed him. But my partner didn't cotton to him at all. Took me aside and started preaching just like Pa used to do. Made me mad. When Thurman saw what Davie was doing, he came over and cussed him out. Told him I was going to ride out with him and if he followed, he was going to get shot."

"Didn't that give you a hint that you'd taken up with bad company?" said Shad. "Or did you care?"

Toby stared at the floor. "I guess I didn't. Not then, anyway. But after awhile I did."

Cornelius poured coffee for everyone and set plates of flapjacks on the sturdy pine table.

"Dig in, if you've a mind to," he invited.

They didn't waste any time. The old hermit sure could cook flapjacks, Shad would give him that.

"Son, what finally made you turn against this Thurman fellow?" Abe asked between bites.

"I found out that they weren't into gold mining. What they were planning to do was steal the gold that others had mined."

"You didn't aim to go along with that, did you?"

Toby looked shocked. "Of course not. I wasn't going to tell 'em outright, though. There was too many of 'em. So when I thought they were asleep, I packed my gear and started to take off. Trouble was Norm Quillen was watching. He yelled for the others. They grabbed me and I ended up a prisoner."

"Then what?"

He looked embarrassed. "Well, I'd been kind of bragging about how me and my old man owned a big cattle ranch up in Colorado. Wanted 'em to think I was somebody, not just a green kid with empty pockets. After they tied me up, they remembered all that and said they were going to hold me for ransom. If Pa didn't come up with the money, they'd kill me. Thurman said they'd have plenty of time before the gold shipment went out."

"How did you get away from them?" asked Shad, knowing that was no small feat.

"Mostly I got lucky. The next night they were feeling real good and talking about how they'd spend the ransom money. From the way Thurman looked at me, though, I knew I didn't have a chance. I was plenty scared. Well, they started passing a bottle around and pretty soon, when that one was empty, they broke out another. Must have been past midnight by the time they were all passed out, drunk as skunks. I managed to get hold of a knife and cut myself loose. Grabbed a rifle and some shells. Then I started for Banjo, but he was too far away, over by where Quillen was bedded down. I was scared to try for him, so I threw a saddle on the closest, that no-account claybank you saw tied outside. I walked him for a long way so they wouldn't hear us and wake up. Then I rode out of there like the devil was on my coattails. Don't think any of 'em stirred, but, come morning, they were sure to.

"I headed toward Davie's place, hoping to make peace with him. Then I figured that'd be the first place they'd look. They'd want me bad. Not only for the ransom, but because I knew what they were planning to do about the gold. They'd talked right in front of me like I was a member of the gang."

"Boy, you sure got yourself into hot water," said Abe.

"I know. I decided to go where they wouldn't think to look and took off the trail before I got to Davie's. I was planning to head for the mining camp the back way. That's when that no-account horse got spooked and threw me. Cornelius found me knocked out cold. He loaded me up and brought me here."

"Well," said Abe, "it was a dumb stunt to pull, hooking up with a pack of outlaws. On top of that you practically invited 'em to hold you for ransom, lying to 'em like you did about being rich. What have you got between your ears, boy? Cornmeal mush?"

Chastened, Toby hung his head.

"Well, I expect one of us had better ride down and warn that Stovall fellow," said Shad. "From all accounts he's a good man, and those outlaws aren't apt to treat him very well when they get there."

"I never thought of that," said Toby. "I don't want nothing to happen to Davie on account of me."

"Then the next time you get a hair-brained notion, stop and think of the trouble it might cause," said Abe.

"Say, was you telling the truth about Pa? I mean, is he really dying?"

Abe stood and put his hand on the boy's shoulder. "Sorry, son. It's true. Nat wanted to see you again before he passed on. He asked Shad to find you and bring you home. The Judge asked me to follow along."

"We had a big fight just before I left."

"All the more reason for you and your pa to make things right before it's too late."

Cornelius had stayed in the background, watching and listening. "He's right, boy. Folks shouldn't part that way, leaving things unsaid. I can tell you that for sure."

While they were trying to convince Toby, Shad had another worry. "The outlaws can't be far behind us. After that lie Thurman told me about Stovall selling the Appaloosa, they'll know we're headed for his place. That's where they'll expect to find Toby, too. If they get there before we do, the man's in big trouble."

Toby turned pale beneath his sunburn. "I've been a fool. We've got to help Davie. It's my fault he's in this mess at all."

Chapter Four

In a haze of cigar smoke, Drake Mohler paced impatiently behind the livery stable. Quillen and Scott had been due back long ago. He had a bad feeling that something had gone wrong. It should have been a simple matter to find that horse thief and the man that had joined him, wait until they were asleep, and shoot them. At least it would have been a simple matter for himself. Now his business in Cimarron was finished, his hangover was gone, and he was ready to pull out. Where in blazes were they?

He looked up to see Red Thurman approaching, with Strong tagging along behind. They were leading their mounts.

"Everything's packed and we're all ready to go," said Strong. "Maybe Quillen and Scott decided to wait for us in the canyon instead of riding all the way back to Cimarron."

Mohler dropped what little remained of the cigar and crushed it under his boot. "Maybe. But I told 'em I wanted to know for sure that fellow was out of the way, and I wanted his horses."

"And I wanted back my pearl-handled Smith and Wesson that he took," said Thurman. "I hate to think it, but maybe him and that other fellow got away from the boys, somehow."

The same notion had been nagging at Mohler. The two he wanted killed were spotted heading for the canyon and their lead wasn't all that big. How could his two gunmen miss?

"Well, if they got 'em, it looks like they'd be back by now unless they'd decided to wait," said Strong.

The logic was unassailable.

"Come on, let's get out of here," Mohler ordered. "Our friend up at Last Chance sent word to Cimarron that he wants to have a little talk."

"Is everything all right, boss?" asked Strong.

"He claims the shipment's going out soon, but he wasn't specific about the day or hour. He probably doesn't know the particulars. But it means we've gotta get our hands on that fool kid before he starts talking to the wrong people."

"So, what do we do now?" asked Thurman.

"I'm not waiting here any longer."

Mohler went inside the livery stable and saddled and bridled his horse. Then the three of them left the trail town behind them in a cloud of dust.

It was the next day that they found Quillen. Foot-sore, he was limping toward town, leading his skewbald gelding. Scott was nowhere in sight. Mohler didn't like it. Not one bit.

"What's happened?" he demanded to know. "Where's Scott?"

Quillen looked sheepish. "Can't rightly say what happened to him. Old Mac, here, got lame on me and Scotty rode on ahead. Said he could handle a couple of greenhorns on his own. Said he'd wait 'til they were asleep and take care of 'em. But then he never came back."

"You gotta put that horse down," said Mohler, glancing at the sorry sight. "For the time being, you can ride one of mine."

Quillen looked sick. It didn't bother him to kill a man, but shooting his own horse was another matter.

"I'll do it," offered Strong. "Go over yonder, Norm. You don't have to look."

Quillen removed his saddle, bridle, and saddlebags. Then he gave the horse a pat and walked off. Strong took out his pistol and fired a couple of quick shots. The lame horse went down. Quillen winced at the sound.

"Get that saddle on the roan," ordered Mohler. "We don't have any more time to stand around waiting on you."

Quillen hurried to obey.

They were deep inside the canyon when they came upon the remains of a campsite. Strong got down and felt the ashes.

"They're cold," he said. "But the camp is recent."

Mohler leaned over the saddle horn in order to read the sign. There had been four of them. Counting Scott as the fourth man, then three. There were also the tracks of a heavily loaded wagon.

"Well, there's no bodies," said Thurman. "But there's some spent shells. Somebody's been doing some shooting."

There was no scattered gear, either, Mohler noted. Only the ashes of the fire, the shells, and a stain of blood on some brush-covered earth.

"Somebody in that outfit took a bullet," he said. "But I'd like to know what happened to Scott."

He glanced around the area with a sense of foreboding. "Climb the flank of the canyon a ways," he ordered Quillen. "Maybe from up there you'll be able to spot something we're missing down here."

Quillen dismounted and scrambled up the sloping side. He hadn't gone far before he stopped in his tracks.

"Boss, I think you'd better come up here and take a look," he called. "There's been some dirt turned over. A lot of it. And it's been done recent."

Mohler and the others climbed the slope to where he waited. Sure enough, someone had made a pile of dirt.

"Well, don't just stand there," he said. "See what's underneath."

Quick to follow orders, Quillen grabbed a stout stick and began raking away the earth covering. Thurman joined in, adding a few vicious kicks. The last of these exposed a piece of blue flannel. He knelt and pulled on it. At the end was a human hand. Scott's hand. Mohler uttered a curse.

"Dumb saddle tramp. Couldn't find his own backside without a lantern. Guess this served him right."

"You've got to admit that Scotty wasn't expecting to find three men," said Strong. "It must have been too many for him."

Strong's excuses aggravated Mohler. "No reason to get himself killed. He should've held back. Waited for a chance to pick 'em off one at a time."

"I wonder who that horse thief went and hooked up

with?" said Quillen. "Boss, do you think he was telling the truth when he said there were others out looking for that kid?"

"How would I know?"

In fact, the question had niggled. How many did that fellow say? Six? Well, here was evidence of three. His main worry was that they'd get to the kid first. When Granger spilled what he knew about the plans for the gold robbery, a fortune would slip away like fog in the sunshine. He kicked himself for not putting a stop to all the loose talk that had gone on in front of the boy. Usually he was more cautious. But the way he'd planned it, once the ransom had been paid, the Granger kid was going to die. No loose ends, just the way he liked it. Then, all of a sudden, everything had gone to blazes. The dumb bunch that worked for him had messed up. Now he was going to have to fix it.

"We've got to get to that Granger kid before them others," he said, staring down at the dead man's arm like it was a coiled rattlesnake. "There's way too much at stake to let him ruin it for us."

"Where do we start lookin'?" asked Thurman.

"I'm betting he'll go right back to that same place where you found him. He'll be wanting to team up with that old prospector again."

"Sounds reasonable. But we'd better get a move on if we want to beat them others to his cabin. Since I set that fellow onto Stovall, they'll be looking for him, too. And if that kid ever starts talking, a lot of people are sure to start asking questions."

No reminder was needed. People got itchy trigger-fingers when they were dealing with gold. And while nobody was apt to take the word of a smart-mouth kid over the assurances of a pompous stuffed-shirt like Clay Todd, the mine supervisor, they'd be sure to remember what he'd said after a gold shipment had disappeared.

"Let's get on with it," Mohler ordered. "We haven't got any more time to waste."

They left Scott's remains as they'd found them and rode west until nightfall.

The next morning, they dropped out of the canyon and entered the valley. Mohler had ridden through it many times before and was familiar with most of it. Today there wasn't a soul in sight, except for a distant cowhand who was checking on some cattle.

"To have gotten through here so quick," said Thurman, "they must've took off and run for it after shooting Scott. Quite a feat with that loaded wagon."

"I'm not worried," said Mohler. "It won't do 'em a bit of good since we know where they're headed. They'll have to find Stovall. He's their only lead."

"It'll make it convenient since the kid's likely gone there, too. We'll get rid of 'em all at the same time."

Mohler found himself smiling for the first time in a long while. "Won't it, though. We're like one of them parades. All lined up and marching down the same road to the same place."

"You two make it sound easy," said Quillen, a note of doubt in his voice.

He shook his head. "Nope. I don't expect anything to be easy. That's like daring Fate to give you a big whack in the jaw. I learned that a long time ago. But we'll get it done. We've got to. There's too much at stake."

They crossed most of the valley and headed north, up into the mountains. Dusk caught them on the trail.

Since they'd replenished their supplies in Cimarron, they'd eat well. They'd drink well, too, but only a little. Mohler didn't need a bunch of drunks in his camp, shooting off their mouths and their guns. Neither did he want his men nursing hangovers the next morning. They all needed to keep their wits about them.

That night, warmly cocooned in his bedroll, he looked up at the stars. This was something he didn't do much anymore except maybe to check the time. *Is a man's destiny written in the stars like some say it is?* He thought about that for a while. *No, that notion is way too lofty. A man takes charge of his own life and determines how it goes, not some pinpoint of light that no one can even touch.* On that reassuring thought, Drake Mohler went to sleep.

Dawn ushered in a clear day with a wind blowing out of the north. They ate a quick meal and saddled up. Thurman, their best tracker, led the way. The trail wound ever upward through firs and aspens. Within the wilderness that surrounded them, there were plenty of places for a man to hide. But they were following wagon tracks, along with the tracks of five horses, two of which had riders.

After a time, Thurman reined up, glanced back at them, and pointed to the ground. "Look," he said. "The wagon and horses stopped here, but only the wagon and team went on ahead."

"Where'd the others go?" asked Mohler.

Thurman dismounted and followed the tracks to the edge of the forest. "Two men on horseback and three other horses took off right here. Why they would do that, I don't know. There's no trail leading off. Nothing."

Mohler was puzzled. It didn't make sense.

"This ain't the way to Stovall's place," said Quillen. "What is it they're up to?"

Mohler wished he knew. It seemed crazy. But tracks don't lie.

"You think they might have gone up there to hide and ambush us?" asked Strong.

Mohler gave him a scathing look. "If they'd had that in mind, I expect we'd all be dead by now."

He climbed down and went to have a closer look for himself. It was plain to see where they'd entered the woods. But why here at this spot? A man could get lost and wander around for days. And what was up there, anyhow?

"What are we going to do now, boss?" asked Quillen.

Mohler was consumed with curiosity. He wanted to follow those tracks in the worst way. But he knew he couldn't afford the time. He had to find Granger and shut him up. Then he had to go meet Todd.

"Let's get a move on," he said, walking back and throwing his leg over the saddle. "We're heading straight for Stovall's place."

Unlike some of the other prospectors, Stovall had built himself a wooden shack, along with some nearby outbuildings. There wasn't much daylight left when Mohler and his men paused to look the place over before riding into the clearing that surrounded it. The old man was there, no doubt about it. Smoke rose from the chimney pipe. In a lean-to off to the side, a mule brayed a warning.

"He'll be armed," warned Thurman. "He's saltier than he looks."

"Don't guess he liked it much when that kid of his took off with you."

"Nope. He had a few things to say about it."

"Thurman, you and Quillen go to opposite sides," ordered Mohler. "Be ready when he comes out."

They got into position. Except for the braying mule, there wasn't a sound. Even the birds were quiet.

"You in there!" yelled Mohler, his .45 drawn. "Come on out here. We want to talk to you."

Silence.

"This is your last chance!"

A shotgun appeared at the window. "Get out of here, you mangy coyotes! All of you! I'll blast your hides if you don't."

"Gutsy, ain't he?" said Mohler. He turned to Strong. "Get up there on the roof and cover the stove pipe with something."

"Right, boss."

Strong circled around to the blind side of the shack and hauled himself up on the roof. Meanwhile, Mohler tried to keep the old man distracted.

"Why don't you make this easy on yourself," he called. "There's four of us and only one of you. That is, unless you're hiding that kid in there. If you are, we want him back. That's what we came here for."

"What happened? He smarten up and pull out on you? Well, he's not here. He wouldn't have the gall to come crawling back, not after the way he went and done me. So you just turn them horses around and go on back where you came from."

Strong was on the roof, covering the vent with his vest. It didn't take long for black smoke to come billowing out of every opening it could find. The door burst open and Stovall came staggering out, coughing and gasping for air. Thurman and Quillen had him covered. Mohler climbed down and grabbed him by the collar.

"All right, old man, where are you hiding the kid?"

Stovall shot him a look of contempt. "I told you he wouldn't come back here. Look around if you don't believe me."

"Search the place!" Mohler ordered.

When they found no sign of Granger, Mohler lost his temper. He turned to the prospector.

"Old man, I think you know where he went. If you want to live a little longer, you're going to tell us."

Stovall stood his ground. "How in blazes should I know where he is? He was just a stray kid who showed up and hung around here for awhile. I let him do a little work for me and fed him in exchange."

Mohler nodded to Thurman who was waiting for his signal. Thurman stepped up and rammed a fist into the old man's gut. He groaned and doubled over. Again and again, Thurman hit him. While he worked Stovall over, the others watched. When he was finished, the old prospector lay in a heap. His face was swollen. Blood ran down his chin.

"All right," said Mohler, "leave him. Time is growing short and we've got more important things to do."

They left the clearing in front of the shack and headed for their hideout near the gold camp. Mohler was worried now. The kid might have gone on back to that ranch of his in Colorado, but the tracks of the stolen claybank had led in the other direction. Had he talked to anyone? More important, had anyone listened?

"Do you reckon Todd's been told exactly when that shipment is leaving, and he's holding out on us?" asked Thurman.

The thought had briefly crossed Mohler's mind, but he'd discounted it. There was no reason for the mine supervisor to hold out any information that he could glean.

"No," he said. "Todd claims he heard that it'll be going out soon. They won't be telling him exactly when until the last minute. The big shots think it adds to the security."

Truth to tell, Mohler didn't have any liking for Todd. The man was a pompous fool. It was galling to have to confess to him a slip-up like Granger. Maybe he wouldn't. Maybe it'd be best not to mention it.

It was dark when they rode up to the abandoned shack they'd taken over. It was closer to the camp than Stovall's place. Todd was supposed to meet them here.

"I don't see hide nor hair of him," said Quillen. "It don't look like anybody's been here since we left."

"Then he'll come tomorrow. His message said he was going to meet with me even if he hadn't got word. We'll wait."

They went inside the abandoned shack. It provided shelter, but just barely.

"I'm still worried about that kid," said Thurman. "If he shoots off his mouth, he could do us a lot of harm."

Mohler struck a match to the tinder in the fireplace and watched it blaze up.

"Why don't you shut up about it. Let me do the worrying."

If any talk of a robbery had gotten back to the mine bosses, Todd would have heard. They'd find out when he arrived. If he hadn't heard anything, then chances were good they were in the clear.

*   *   *

Davie Stovall lay sprawled on the ground. He was hurting in every bone, and unable to move. It took him a minute to remember why he was out in the open with the taste of blood and dirt in his mouth. A moan escaped him. Out of swollen eyes he could see the stars. They looked cold and far away. He shivered. He had to get inside to shelter. Had that outlaw broken anything? He tried and found he was able to move his left arm. Gently he felt his ribs. Must be at least a couple that were cracked or broken, he decided. Holding one arm across his injured ribs, he struggled to his knees. By inches, he scooted himself across the open space to the shack. Once inside, he closed the door. Then, pulling himself up on the bunk, he covered up with blankets and slept.

It was daylight when he awoke. Pain still wracked his body. The red-headed outlaw had worked him over good. He licked his cracked lips; his mouth was dry as sand. The day before, he'd filled the water bucket. There ought to be some still in it. He hauled himself from the bed. On unsteady feet he shuffled over and filled the dipper. Nothing had ever tasted so good as that first mouthful of water. After satisfying his thirst, he eased himself back on the bunk to rest some more. When a little of his strength had returned, he reached over and cut an old blanket into strips and bound his rib cage. What internal damage had been done, he couldn't tell. Nothing to do but rest. Maybe hot tea and broth would help. Tea was supposed to be good for shock. He'd get around to trying it later. But when it came right down to it, he'd either live or he wouldn't. From outside came a plaintive bray. The door was pushed open and the mule poked his head inside.

"Whiskey, you old son of a gun," Stovall said, delighted that the outlaws hadn't stolen his old pal. "You must've run off when all that ruckus was going on."

Whiskey came on inside and Davie patted his nose.

"There's water down at the stream and plenty of grass for you to munch on. You're just going to have to take care of yourself for awhile until I can get back on my feet."

The mule nodded as if he understood.

"Now, get on out," he said. "There's not room inside here for both of us."

Satisfied that he hadn't been abandoned, Whiskey obliged and went looking for his breakfast.

Stovall lay back and thought about the kid he'd taken in. Why was that bunch of no-accounts so anxious to get their hands on him? What did he have that they wanted? Maybe it wasn't what he had. Maybe it was what he knew. Toby was a likable boy, and Stovall had taken to him from the start. Most likely he was a fool, but a man alone sometimes welcomes company, and he enjoyed having him around. He'd known from the start that he wouldn't stay long. The boy was too restless. But he'd hated like poison to see him go off with that Thurman fellow. It was plain to anyone who cared to look that Thurman had a mean streak. Anyway, he hoped that Toby was a long ways off, maybe back at that ranch he used to talk about. One thing was for sure, if he wasn't, and the outlaws got their hands on him, he was finished.

He needed a weapon in case they came back. They'd taken the old Winchester when they rode out, but they might not have spared the time to search the shack with any thoroughness. He got up and looked underneath the bunk. Hidden by the drop of blankets was a shelf. On that shelf was a Spencer carbine and next to it was plenty of ammunition. First, he checked to make sure he'd loaded it. Then he placed it on his bed. If they decided to come back for another go-round, he'd be ready for them.

The next morning, Mohler watched as Todd rode up the trail on that fancy sorrel he was so proud of. The others were waiting back in the hideout. This was between him and Todd. The mine supervisor was dressed in black pants and a black shield-type shirt with pearl buttons. His hat looked new and so did his boots. The man had expensive taste. Nothing down at the heel for that dandy. He was all-fired proud of his looks, too. He was waited until Todd was almost upon him before he rode from the screen of trees, directly into his path. The sorrel shied and Todd cursed.

"Mohler, don't you ever jump out at me like that again!" he barked.

Mohler bit back a reply. *One of these days*, he thought. *One of these days you'll get what's coming to you.*

"Well, when's the shipment going out?" he said, keeping himself under control.

Todd gave him an icy look. "Sometime within the next few days, if I read the signs right. As soon as I get the order, I'll let you know. I'm expecting you to do your part and do it right. You're getting paid well enough, that's for sure."

Mohler decided to give Todd something to worry about. He deserved it.

"I'm afraid there's been a little problem. We had this kid with us for a time. About sixteen, he was. Well, he overheard the others talking about robbing the gold shipment. Then one night, he up and took off. We've been hunting for him, but we haven't been able to find him. At least not yet."

Todd turned red in the face and gave him a murderous look.

"Of all the dumb stunts. Find him! He could ruin everything."

His reaction gave Mohler considerable satisfaction.

"That's what me and my men have been trying to do, like I told you. It's possible that he went back to his ranch in Colorado. He won't give us any trouble from up there."

"Maybe not in time to stop us. But he can certainly get a lot of the wrong people to ask questions. When this is done with, you're going to have to find him, wherever he is, and clean up your blunder."

Mohler nodded. "We'll take care of it later. But if he comes into Last Chance running off his mouth, it'll be up to you to do something about it."

"What's he look like?"

Mohler had no trouble recalling. "Big raw-boned kid with light hair the color of straw. A nose that's sunburnt. And freckles. He's got a lot of freckles."

"I'll be on the lookout. Meanwhile, you and your men get ready. My man, Bledsoe, will drive the wagon and I'll send along as few guards as I can get away with."

"We'll do our part."

Mohler watched Todd wheel the sorrel and ride back toward the mining camp. Then he took a cigar from his pocket, clipped the end, and lit it with a match. Small pleasures, such as good tobacco, compensated for a lot of unpleasantness, like a pompous mine supervisor who thought he was a cut above the ordinary.

He wondered how much gold would be in the shipment. Todd hadn't said, but it was sure to be a lot. Split five ways it would be enough to make them all rich. Split fewer ways, it would make the ones that were left even richer. Split not at all, it would mean a vast fortune. No doubt Todd had thought of this, too. The man was a weasel and not to be trusted. Mohler decided he'd have to take care of him when the time was right, and when the gold was safely in his own hands.

Chapter Five

Shad sat across the pine plank table from Abe. The aroma of the hermit's flapjacks was making his mouth water. The coffee smelled pretty good, too. He dug in with enthusiasm.

He noticed the look of concern on his old friend's face despite the fine meal he was sharing. Toby was perched on a nearby stool, his expression sullen. Cornelius, the hermit, hovered in the background. He watched and listened but didn't intrude.

As Shad set about devouring the honey-coated stack of cakes, he thought about how a man could get himself caught between two duties that each pulled him in a different direction. There was Nat back at the ranch fighting for every day, if not for every heartbeat. He wanted nothing more than to see his son again before he had to let go of life. But now that they'd found his boy, Shad was faced with a dilemma. No way could they ride off and leave Toby's friend to the cruelty of the outlaws. Nor could they go back to Colorado and let Mohler and

59

his gang make off with a gold shipment. Knowing Abe as he did, his partner would feel the same way. Added to all of this was the fact that they couldn't trust Toby to make the journey home by himself. Any way you looked at it, this was a bad state of affairs.

He ate the last bite and drained the coffee cup. Breakfast was good, at least.

"Have some more," invited Cornelius, refilling his cup. "I've been hearing talk about this Mohler outfit. The way it's told, they've robbed a prospector here and there. Stole a few horses. Nothing real big. But I doubt if they'd think twice about killing a man. It's not a good idea for a fellow to get crosswise of 'em."

Shad recalled how Cornelius had shot at them the day before. But since he was trying to scare them off, not kill them, he figured it was best to let bygones be bygones. He'd consider the flapjacks a peace offering. As to the outlaws, the decision was already made.

"I'm going to ride over to that gold camp and warn them about Mohler."

Toby jumped up and slammed the flat of his hand on the table. "I knew it! I knew you was lying! If Pa was in a bad way like you said, you wouldn't be worrying about somebody else's gold."

Shad gave him a blistering look.

Abe put his fork down. "Son," he said, "we've been telling you the way it is. Your pa has sent us to bring you home 'cause he's not got long before meeting his Maker. Might even be gone already as we sit here jawin'. If so, you're going to feel real bad about that when you grow up to be a man."

Toby's face turned red at the put-down. "Why, you old coot, I am a man! A better man than you are."

Shad started from his chair, but Abe warned him off with a gesture and stood up.

"Toby," he said, looking him straight in the eye, "your pa taught you to behave better. Nobody calls me an old coot and gets away with it. Nor a liar, neither."

Before the kid knew what hit him, he was flat on the floor staring up at the rafters. Shad and Cornelius looked on.

"Man's right," said the hermit. "Fellow ought to respect his elders."

When Toby recovered from the shock of being decked by a lifelong friend, he slowly got to his feet.

"Sorry," he said. "Guess I wasn't thinking."

"I guess you wasn't," said Abe.

"You really don't believe they'd go back to Davie Stovall's place and hurt him, do you?"

That he was concerned about Stovall was encouraging.

"Son, you rode with 'em. What do you think?"

Toby got his point and looked sick. "Guess we'd better go see about him. I'll show you the way."

Cornelius gathered the empty plates. "How much of a lead did you have on them outlaws?"

"My guess is not a whole lot," said Shad. "Maybe a day. A couple at most. Depends on how long they stayed in Cimarron. We need to get the horses took care of and then we'll head out."

Abe collected the black with the blaze and the big gray, along with the horse that had belonged to Scott. Shad took care of the dun, handing the Appaloosa over to Toby. The kid also had the outlaw's horse that he'd escaped on.

When they were ready to leave, Cornelius stood in the doorway looking regretful.

"You fellows be careful," he warned. "And remember, you're always welcome here. I'm sorry as can be that I shot at you."

"Much obliged for your hospitality," said Abe.

They made their way down from the hermit's aerie in silence, this time taking a more direct route. Shad admitted to himself that he liked Cornelius. He seemed to enjoy company a lot more than most of his kind. But why was he hiding up there, apart from his fellows? He knew that some did it for religious reasons, but Cornelius didn't seem to fit that group. Sometimes when a man was hiding from the law, or from something else, he took himself away like that. He was betting that Cornelius was hiding from something else, since he didn't seem the outlaw type. Whatever it was, it was his own business.

It was afternoon by the time Toby led them to the edge of a small clearing. Before them stood a prospector's shack with a few outbuildings nearby. The ground had been churned by horses' hooves. A bad sign.

"Something's wrong!" said Toby, alarmed at the sight.

He flung himself off the Appaloosa, ran to the shack, and shoved the door open. Shad and Abe were a couple of steps behind him. They found Toby's friend, Stovall, asleep on his bunk. What they could see of him was covered in bruises, and his eyes were black and swollen. A makeshift bandage circled his ribs.

"Mohler and that outfit of his have been here already," said Toby, his voice anguished. "Look how they worked him over. He didn't stand a chance and it's all my fault."

"Let's see what we can do for him," said Abe.

Stovall opened his eyes. At least as much as he could get them open.

"Toby? You came back?"

Toby knelt beside him. "Yeah. I'm sorry I left in the first place," he said softly. "Most of all I'm sorry they came here and did this to you all because of me."

"They want you real bad, son. They mean to kill you. You must know something they don't want told around."

"Here, let me see what I can do for you," said Abe, gently pushing Toby aside.

He removed the makeshift blanket rags that circled the injured man's ribs. Then he washed him down. Finally, be took some clean strips of bandage that he carried in his supplies and rebound the rib area. Stovall groaned.

"Put some water on for tea," Abe ordered. "Nothing's better for shock. I've got some laudanum, too. It'll ease the pain."

When Abe was through with his doctoring, Davie Stovall sat up and looked at Toby.

"They came here to get you, Toby. When they couldn't find you, they tried to make me tell 'em where you were holed up."

"I'm real sorry about this, Davie," Toby said, his voice shaky. "I'm going to get 'em for what they done to you. I swear I will."

Shad heard a noise outside and cracked the door to look. "Someone's out there."

"Where?" asked Toby, rushing to his side.

"In the trees, just beyond the clearing."

Shad hefted his rifle. Abe picked up his shotgun and went over to the window.

"Whoever you are out there, ride in carefully!" called Shad. "Keep your hands in sight and don't make any sudden moves."

"It's me, Lark Russell!" came the reply.

"Well, I'll be . . ." said Abe.

Sure enough, the female teamster came riding into the clearing, bold as you please, on a handsome blood bay mare. Abe hurried out to greet her.

"I was so worried about Davie," she explained when they got to the shack. "I left the team and wagon back at Last Chance and rode up here to check on him. He's an old friend of my father."

"Thank your stars you didn't get here sooner, Miss Lark," said Abe. "You'd have run into the Mohler gang. While we were at the hermit's place rounding up this wayward boy, they hightailed it up here to find Stovall and worked him over pretty good."

She looked past them to the bunk, her expression one of alarm. "Davie, are you all right?" There was no pretense of being a man. Her voice was normal.

"I've been better, Larkspur. Got some ribs broke and a lot of bruises, but I'll live."

"You didn't see any sign of them coyotes between here and the camp, did you?" asked Abe.

"No. But then I doubt if they'd ride into Last Chance, or anywhere close. Mohler is notorious in these parts. He'd be spotted right off."

Shad left her and the others and went outside. The shack was getting too crowded for comfort. Besides, he hated standing around. Toby followed him.

"Wouldn't be a bad lookin' woman if she was gussied up a little," the kid observed. "Appears that Abe's taken a shine to her."

"Maybe. If he has, it's his business and none of ours."

"Well, I hope she don't hurt him. That's all I care about."

Shad cared about that too. Still, it wasn't any of his business.

Inside, Lark got busy cooking. When the soup and cornbread were ready, she called them all together. While they ate, Shad asked her about the gold camp.

"Who is it that I should talk to in Last Chance about this robbery business?"

She considered the question. "I guess it would be Clay Todd. He's pretty much in charge in the absence of the mine owners."

"What kind of law does Last Chance have?"

"Todd, I suppose, and whoever he appoints as his security officer. He's really the mine supervisor, but he runs the camp like it was his own little kingdom."

It was a set-up that Shad didn't like. Autocratic men were rarely honest ones. Maybe Todd was different. It might be that a place like Last Chance needed a firm hand.

"Think I'll take a ride over there and have a little talk with this fellow. He ought to be told what's in store for that gold shipment."

"I'll go with you," said Toby.

"No. You stay here and help Abe and Miss Lark. I don't want to call any more attention to myself than I have to. Besides, those outlaws may decide to come back. If they do, you'll be needed."

It was plain to see that the boy was disappointed, but to his credit, he didn't argue.

Shad took his leave. Riding the dun, he made his way

generally north, all the while following the curve of the mountain. Last Chance was only a few miles distant as the crow flies. Unfortunately, Squire didn't have wings.

It was late evening when he came to an overlook. From this vantage point, he could see the gold camp below—at least all but the stamp mill, which, because of its noise, would be located some distance away. The houses were nestled in a clearing, surrounded by pines. The community was comprised of thirty or more wooden structures, not counting the outbuildings.

"Well, let's go down and see how things shape up," he said to Squire.

As he rode into Last Chance, it appeared to be deserted. The men were off working in the mine or the mill, he supposed. The place was likely short on women, for few would care to live in this remote location. He paused and looked around. For some reason, he felt edgy. Something wasn't right. This was the same feeling that he sometimes got when trouble was about to start.

A scrappy little dog crawled out from under the foundation of a shack and started yapping at him. The noise brought a scrawny-looking boy of about ten from around the corner of a building, a smaller version of himself in tow.

"Hush up, Rags," he ordered. The dog reluctantly obeyed, maintaining a low growl.

"Rags always barks at strangers," the boy explained.

"Good watchdog," said Shad. "Can you tell me where I can find Mr. Todd?"

"Sure. He rode into town a little while ago. He's over there at his place right now." The boy pointed to a structure that was larger than the others. "That's where he lives, and where his office is too."

"Obliged," Shad said, tossing the boy a coin.

He rode over and tied his horse in front of the superintendent's house. Then he stepped up on the porch and knocked sharply on the door. After a minute's wait, it was opened by a heavy-set woman with a dour expression.

"What is it you want?" she said, looking him over as if he were a specimen under a microscope, one that she didn't especially care to be seeing.

"Would you be Mrs. Todd?" he inquired politely.

She glared at him. "No, I ain't. I'm the housekeeper."

"It's important that I speak to Mr. Todd right away. The name's Shad Wakefield."

"Wait here," she ordered, and shut the door in his face.

Rude woman. She wouldn't last a day in the Judge's household.

A few minutes passed before she was back.

"Mr. Todd will see you, but make it quick. He ain't got time to waste on every saddle bum that happens to stop by."

Shad bit back a sharp retort and followed the housekeeper as she waddled down the hall to Todd's office.

"Here he is," she announced. Then she turned on her heel, leaving him to enter the room and make his own introduction.

Todd glanced up and eyed Shad with suspicion. He was a pale man with thin lips and thinning blond hair.

"Well, what is it you want?" he demanded. "You don't look like a miner to me."

Shad had been given no invitation to sit in one of the leather-covered chairs that flanked the desk. The house-keeper had been rude. Todd was even ruder.

"You're quite right," said Shad, "I'm not a miner. I'm an attorney and a rancher. The reason I'm here is to warn you that your next gold shipment is going to be robbed by the Mohler gang. I thought you'd like to know so you can be ready for them."

Todd reacted to his statement like he'd been slapped. His small eyes squinched to slits. His expression was livid.

"Who else have you been telling this ridiculous story to?" he demanded.

"Is that important?" Shad asked, puzzled by the superintendent's peculiar reaction.

Todd's hand came up from behind the desk. It held a gun and that gun was pointed at Shad. He stood and yelled for the housekeeper. When she appeared, he ordered, "Tilda, get Bledsoe over here quick. Run!"

His eyes never wavered from Shad. "Don't move," he said, "or I'll kill you."

Todd then eased himself around the desk and lifted Shad's pistol from its holster.

"Now, I'm going to show you what I do with your kind."

Shad had a sick feeling. It was all too clear now. Mohler was only the hired hand. Todd was the master-mind. And like a fool, he'd walked right into Todd's gunsight. The inside information the gang needed was coming from the mine supervisor himself.

There was the sound of heavy footsteps running down the hall. A stocky man with a red, bulbous nose burst into the room. He was panting from his exertion.

"What is it, Mr. Todd?" he gasped.

"Take this thief, here, and lock him in one of the sheds. I caught him red-handed pilfering the house."

Bledsoe stared at Shad curiously.

Was the security officer in on this too? He wondered. Shad had to take a chance that he wasn't.

"What would I pilfer?" he asked. "There's nothing here of value. I came here to warn Todd that the Mohler gang is going to rob the gold shipment."

Todd gave the security officer a nod. Bledsow turned and felled Shad with a strong right jab. He was down on his knees, gasping for air, when Bledsoe kicked him hard.

"Drag him off and lock him up in the shed before he gets a chance to talk to anyone else," ordered Todd.

His body hurting, Shad tried to stagger to his feet. Bledsoe kicked him in the head. This time, he blacked out.

It was dark when the thick blanket of mist began to lift. Shad's ribs ached and his head throbbed. On top of that, he felt like he'd been kicked in the stomach by a mule. His mouth was dry as a sandstorm and he could barely swallow. Wherever he was, it wasn't only dark, it was cold. He struggled to his knees and crawled along the dirt floor. All the while, he felt around blindly for something to wrap himself in for warmth. Rags, newspapers, anything. The place smelled of damp earth and decayed wood. Most likely, he was locked in a storage shed. Off to one side, he discovered a pile of rubbish. Gingerly he examined it by feel and discovered a burlap sack. Two of them. Some empty tin cans. A piece of metal. He ran his hand across the cold firmness of the metal. It was a pick with a broken handle that no one had taken the time to fix. An ember of hope flared. Since the floor was dirt, maybe he could dig his way out before daylight. That was when they were sure to come back for him. Ignoring his pain and thirst, he set to work. Using the broken tool, he dug. A hole started to appear beside the wall opposite the door. Then, with one end of the pick, he scooped dirt from beneath the flimsy foundation. He was little more than halfway through when a dog barked in the distance. He froze and listened.

"Shut your yapping, you mangy mongrel!" yelled a man whose sleep had been disturbed. This was followed by the thud of a heavy object like a boot. The noise stopped. Shad released the breath he'd been holding.

Desperation is a hard taskmaster, and he worked without pausing to rest. After a lot of exertion, he managed to gouge an opening large enough to squeeze his body through. He got down and wiggled out of his prison into the cold, dark night. His first view of the stars told him it was a little past midnight. There wasn't much time left, for miners were early risers. First, he needed a weapon. The pear-handed Smith and Wesson that he'd taken from one of Mohler's gang was in his saddlebag. But could he find it? He also needed his horse. Keeping to the shadows, he made his way to the barn-like structure near the corral. Inside, he struck a match and found his saddle and saddlebags thrown over a rail. He blew out the match and retrieved the Smith and Wesson. At least he was armed now. A quick check told him that the gun was still loaded. He stuffed it in his belt and hefted the saddlebags to one shoulder.

Then he took his saddle and a bridle, and made straight for the corral.

Softly he called Squire's name. The dun trotted over and nuzzled his shirt. Shad unlatched the gate, went inside, and saddled his horse. When he was mounted, he opened the corral gate wide. Slapping the nearest horse on the rump, he started them all to running. Squire kept in the lead. He was at the outer edge of the camp when there were shouts. He kept on going. Shots were fired in the darkness, but he was a shadowy figure that was quickly out of range. With their horses gone, the miners wouldn't be able to follow. Neither would Todd and his henchman. At least not for a while.

The first hint of dawn found Shad deep in the forest. He was sore from the beating and chilled to the bone. His teeth chattered from the cold.

"We'd better stop for a while, boy. I don't think I can stay in the saddle much longer."

He climbed down and gathered fuel for a small fire. After adding some tinder that he carried in his supplies, he fumbled for a match. Before long, he had a campfire going. He was thankful for the canteen of water and the packet of coffee that he'd brought. Coffee would help to thaw him even more than the campfire. First he had to warm up. Then he'd ride back to Stovall's place. He had to warn Lark and the others about Todd.

Chapter Six

Todd was startled out of a deep sleep by the sound of gunfire. He flung the covers back and ran to the window clad only in his nightshirt. The room was uncomfortably cold. Outside, it was too dark to see much, but he heard yelling, followed by more shots. Throwing on a dressing gown, he hurried to the front door.

"Bledsoe!" he bellowed, spotting his security man nearby.

"Coming, Boss!" Bledsoe yelled, running toward the house. He was wearing nothing but a union suit and was hopping around whenever his bare feet found sharp stones.

"What in the world is going on?" Todd demanded.

The panting Bledsoe began to blurt out the story. "It's the prisoner. He escaped from that shed and ran off all the horses."

Todd couldn't believe his ears. "How did he escape? Why weren't you out there checking on him? Why didn't you post a guard?"

"I did check on him from time to time," Bledsoe whined. "And you didn't want anybody guarding him for fear he'd talk to 'em."

Bledsoe's excuses only served to enrage Todd further. Wakefield had escaped and there was no telling how much trouble he'd end up causing.

All at once the shooting stopped, and the sudden quiet was a shock to the ears. The miners spotted Todd standing in the doorway and they headed toward him as a group.

"It's all right!" he yelled. "Go on back to bed. I'll take care of everything."

They dispersed to go back to their warm beds as they were told. When they were gone, Todd turned to Bledsoe. "All right, just how did Wakefield get out?"

His second in command shrugged. "I don't know. I haven't had a chance to go look. But I can tell you this, when I threw him in that shed, he was dead to the world. What's more, the door was bolted and there was no way for him to get out without an axe."

Todd swore softly. The man was a dimwit.

Bledsoe sensed that he was in deep trouble and started trying to redeem himself. "You want me to take some men and go after him once we get the horses rounded up?"

That was the last thing in the world Todd wanted. If Wakefield got a chance to talk to those miners, some of them might believe him. After the robbery, they'd all remember and believe.

"No," he said. "It's too late now. I'll handle this."

"Then I'm going back to bed."

He stood watching as Bledsoe retreated into the night. Why had he kept that bungling saddle bum on for so long, he wondered. Of course the answer was because Bledsoe didn't think too much, and from time to time he managed to be useful.

Back inside, Todd considered his problem. Wakefield hadn't been given the chance to talk, at least not to anyone in the camp. Mohler and his outfit were standing by to carry out their orders. The mine owners expected the gold to go out on schedule. So far, nothing had changed. Bledsoe would drive the wagon. There would have to be guards. He figured that four was the least he could get away with sending. After the job was finished, he'd have Mohler and his men hunt down Wakefield, along with that fool kid Mohler had told him about. With them out of the way, Todd was most likely in the clear. But just in case, there was a backup plan.

After the robbery, the furious mine owners would be relentless in their investigation. He had no doubt of that. They might be suspicious of their own mine supervisor, even if they never came across Wakefield and the kid. But gold was power. Once he got his hands on it, he could go anywhere—San Francisco, St. Louis, or perhaps New Orleans. If necessary, he could cross the ocean to Europe. Right away, he'd change his name, create a new past. A man could change his appearance too. Darken his hair, grow a beard. In any city in the world, it would be a simple matter to get lost in the crowd.

As he considered it, Todd came to the conclusion that it might not be smart to wait around, hoping for the best. He had to face it. He would doubtless be suspected. If anything went wrong, not only would he lose a fortune, he'd end up spending years in the Territory prison. He made up his mind. As soon as the gold wagon pulled out, he'd pack what little he wanted to take with him and ride out too. He'd follow at a distance and keep an eye on things. Mohler had revealed himself to be an ambitious thief with big ideas. Only a fool would trust him. Todd was nobody's fool.

He stropped his razor, shaved, and got dressed. Then he went toward the kitchen. It was growing lighter outside. Tilda was there in a faded wrapper, her hair done in two long braids down her back. The room smelled of bacon, eggs, and fresh-brewed coffee. His housekeeper had gotten up, anticipating his needs. It was a shame she wasn't younger and better looking. He'd scarcely finished eating when there was a knock at the door.

"I'll see who it is," said Tilda, hurrying to the front of the house.

Todd heard mumbled voices. Then Tilda led Bledsoe into the kitchen. The sight of him was an irritant.

"What is it now?" he asked.

Bledsoe stood before him, hat in hand, looking awkward and not a little frightened.

"Boss, some of the men are nosing around out there. They're asking questions about what happened last night. They want to know who that prisoner was and why he was a prisoner in the first place. They found the big hole that he dug in the floor of that shed. I told 'em he was a thief, but the way they're acting, it's plain that some of 'em aren't buying that story."

Todd wiped his mouth on a worn napkin and got up from the table. "You get out there and tell 'em again. This time make it convincing. Tell 'em we were going to lock him up for awhile to teach him a lesson. Then we were going to turn him loose. He decided not to wait around. That's all there is to it."

Bledsoe shifted his weight from one foot to the other and looked doubtful.

"Maybe they'll accept that," he said, but clearly he didn't believe it. He started to leave, then stopped.

"By the way, Boss, some of the horses came back and a couple of fellows saddled 'em and went out to round up the others."

"And not you?" Todd asked mildly.

Bledsoe flushed. "Well, after all, I'm the security officer. It's my duty to stay here and guard the camp."

Todd fixed him with a stare. "Of course. Like you were doing when Wakefield rode in, big as you please, and made himself at home in my office."

It gave him a measure of satisfaction to watch Bledsoe squirm.

"Go on," he ordered, his voice cold as ice. "Get out of here."

The security man fled the kitchen. Todd eased his weight out of the chair and followed. He watched from the doorway as Bledsoe crossed the clearing. Just as he started to close the door and go back for the last of the coffee, a rider reined up in front. Todd recognized the lanky fellow with long, tied-back hair as a messenger from the mine bosses. There was a coil of fear in his stomach. Lurvey was shrewd, and he could smell trouble a mile away.

"Mr. Todd," he said, swinging down from the saddle, "I've come to bring you the order that the gold shipment is to go out today."

Todd swallowed hard and tried to keep his hands

from shaking. So this was it. The event he'd been working toward for almost a year.

"Come on inside," he invited in a voice that was
almost steady. "As you can see, we've had a little disturbance, but nothing of any importance."

"Disturbance?"

"Just a petty thief who got away and scattered the
horses."

"Best not let the word 'thief,' petty or otherwise, get
back to the bosses. Makes 'em nervous as a bridegroom
at the church."

Todd felt that he'd been criticized, but there was
nothing he could do about it.

"What are the details of the orders?" he asked,
changing the subject.

"The gold is to be shipped out to Denver today.
You're to send along men to guard it. Pay 'em extra if
need be. If anything happens . . . Well, don't ask. But if
that gold doesn't get to Denver, you'd better light out
for Mexico and you'd better have a fast horse."

Todd bristled at the insinuation. *Did they suspect*?

"Let me take care of my job," he said in his haughti-
est voice. "You stick to worrying about your own."

The messenger glared at him. "Look, Todd, relaying
your orders happens to be my job. You'd be wise to
heed 'em."

When Lurvey was gone, Todd slammed his fist into
the wall, not caring about the pain. He was fed up with
the mine bosses and their lackeys. But Mexico wasn't a
bad idea. A man of means could live down there very
well. One thing was for sure: when that gold shipment
disappeared, he'd better disappear right along with it.

Tilda was suddenly standing in front of him. Her homely face had a worried look.

"Is anything wrong, Mr. Todd?" she asked.

"No," he assured her. "Nothing's wrong. Just go on back to your work."

The last thing he wanted was to have Tilda nosing around, watching his every move. *Keep steady*, he told himself. *You're smart and a step ahead of everyone else.* He went to his office and strapped on his pistol. Next, he pulled his duster on to cover it. Finally, he picked up his rifle and his hat. He'd have to give the order for the gold to be loaded and for the wagon to move out.

In the kitchen he filled a canteen from the water bucket. Tilda had stepped out the back, so he cut a piece of gingerbread that she'd baked the day before. Hurriedly, he wrapped it in a clean napkin. But before he could make his escape, the back door flew open and his housekeeper came clomping in.

"You riding out somewhere, Mr. Todd?" she asked.

He liked her cooking, but not her eternal prying into his business. Still, he didn't want her to become suspicious.

"Yes, but not far. They failed to find a couple of the horses, so I thought I'd take a look around."

"Will you be back for dinner?"

"I don't know, Tilda. Don't do anything special. If I'm here, I'll eat whatever it is you have ready."

With rifle in hand, he went out and relayed the order for the men to load the gold. He named the ones he'd chosen to serve as escort guards. Then he glanced over at the corral. Most, if not all, of the horses had been returned. As a rule, he ordered one of the boys to saddle his mount. But, again, the less attention he attracted, the better. He walked over to the corral and saddled one of the finer horses. Then, trying not to look furtive, he mounted up and headed for the slope.

When he was high above Last Chance, he reined up. From this vantage point, he looked over the mining camp below. There was still a flurry of activity as the miners rushed about to carry out his orders.

Todd was uneasy. He didn't like it that things weren't going exactly as he'd planned. The unexpected could happen, and it had, starting with Mohler's big mouth. That had resulted in Wakefield's visit, which nearly ruined everything. He'd planned to kill Wakefield, but that idiot Bledsoe had let him escape. Wakefield knew that the gold shipment was to be robbed, and so did some wet-behind-the-ears kid. How many others knew? Certainly more than two.

He considered going to that prospector's place where Mohler had thought the kid might return. But Mohler had failed to find him there. No telling where he'd gone off to. Todd decided that it didn't matter anyway. This leak was like a tiny hole in a dike that was growing bigger and bigger. In every venture there was a degree of risk. Mohler had added to his risk substantially. The big outlaw didn't know it, but Todd was going to make him pay.

He waited until he saw the guarded wagon pull out of Last Chance. Then he turned and headed for the outlaws' hideout. He had to get word to them. There was no time to waste.

Before things had started going wrong, he'd thought it wise to stay on at Last Chance after the robbery. At least long enough so as not to arouse suspicion. That wasn't going to be possible now. They were already suspicious. The way Lurvey had looked at him made that clear. But then after two cold, isolated mountain winters, almost anyplace else would be a pleasant change.

When he got close to the hideout, he called out to them, "It's me, Todd!"

Mohler appeared in the doorway. "Ride on in," he said. "We've been waiting for you. We're all ready."

Todd sat his horse in the center of the cabin's small clearing while Mohler and his men came outside.

"The wagon pulled out a little while ago," he said. "We've gone over this before. You know where you're to intercept them."

"How many guards?" asked Mohler.

"Four. Bledsoe is going to be driving. He's with me and he won't give you any trouble. Don't kill him. You might be able to use him. But kill the guards. All of them."

Mohler grinned. Todd was repulsed. Those missing teeth made the outlaw look like a malevolent clown.

"Killing the guards goes without saying," said Mohler. "Me and my men know our business."

"All right, what do you do after you take charge of the gold shipment?"

"We hightail it through the valley and the canyon. Then we hide the wagon inside that old barn this side of Cimarron. If something happens and we can't do that, then we have contacts in town. All of us know who they are."

Red Thurman stepped forward.

"Well, what is it?" said Todd.

"I was thinking that once the word goes out, they'll

be combing this whole area from the Rio Grande to Kansas. They're sure to find the wagon."

Todd glared at him. "Let's hope for all our sakes that they don't."

"The big-shot mine supervisor here is going to see that the gold is divided up and moved out before anything like that happens," said Mohler. "Isn't that right?"

The tone of his voice left little doubt that he was mocking Todd. But this was no time for a confrontation. Todd would take care of the big oaf later.

"You'd better get a move on if you want to be in place to meet the gold wagon," he said. Then he added the lie that he'd made up. "I've got to get on back, now. It'll look strange if I'm away from the camp for too long."

Let them think he was going back to Last Chance, trusting them to do the job and secure the cargo. In fact, he intended be right behind them.

"You leave everything to us," said Mohler. "This is going to work out just like we planned it."

Todd noticed that Mohler had promoted himself in importance. The plan, all of it, had been his own. Mohler was nothing but a two-bit outlaw he'd hired.

While they gathered their horses, Todd rode off on his own. He was relieved to get away from the smell of unwashed bodies and dirty clothes. He could tell they'd been drinking some too. A fact he didn't like, since a job of this importance demanded sobriety. As soon as he was out of sight of the hideout, he hid among the trees and waited for them to leave.

He wasn't about to let Mohler, or Wakefield, or anyone else spoil his one chance to have the kind of life he wanted. It had been a long haul from punching cows and selling magic elixir to store clerk and bank clerk, and finally to mine superintendent. With that gold, he could go to Mexico and live like a Spanish Don. Or maybe to San Francisco, where he'd buy a fine house up on Nob Hill. Or who knew where.

He let the outlaws gain a big lead. Then he followed, taking care to hold back so they didn't spot him. They had made their own path through the wilderness. It was a shortcut to the trail. Fallen pine needles cushioned the way.

It was much later when he saw the others.

"What in blazes . . ." he said aloud.

Most of his view was blocked by trees and the riders were some distance away, so he couldn't tell who they were. What he did know for sure was that it wasn't Mohler and his men. *What else could go wrong?* Todd was torn between anger and despair. Anger won out. He'd learned a long time ago that whenever something went wrong, you fixed it. It was as simple as that. With his rifle balanced across his knees, he nudged the gelding in its sides. He'd have to get a little closer in order to put things right.

Chapter Seven

Shad had huddled close to the small fire, drawing warmth from the flames. It had been a long, miserable night. His head still ached from where Bledsoe had kicked it, and he was tired and sore. In the east, the sun was coming up. He couldn't afford to linger. Squire waited patiently nearby, nibbling on grass.

He was certain that Todd had intended to come back to that shed and kill him the first chance he got. It wouldn't have been hard for him to come up with a plausible excuse, and who in Last Chance would doubt the mine supervisor's word? He'd had a narrow escape, and he knew he was lucky to be alive.

Reluctantly, he got to his feet and stretched the aching muscles in his back and legs. A bird on a nearby branch was noisily welcoming the sun. The cool morning breeze jostled the pine needles. It made a soothing, whispering sound.

Shad's thoughts turned to the ranch in Colorado. If Nat hadn't sent him on this journey, he'd be back there, right now, taking care of business. Instead, he was shivering beside a dying fire on a remote mountainside. But debts had to be paid, and he intended to repay Nat Granger for saving his life.

Running off the horses at Last Chance had bought him some time. Pursuit would be delayed, perhaps abandoned. Todd couldn't afford to have him talking to any of the miners. Even if they'd refused to believe him, Shad would have planted suspicion in their minds. Then after the robbery, they'd remember what he'd said and Todd's neck would be in a noose.

Something nagged at him, though. If Mohler told Todd about Toby, and that the kid had learned of the plan to steal the gold, then everyone at Stovall's place could be in danger. If not before the robbery, then certainly afterward.

"Come on, boy," he said to Squire, "we've got some miles to cover."

Shad put his foot in the stirrup and threw his leg over the saddle. Then he headed for the prospector's shack. When at last he rode up to the clearing, he was spotted right off. Both Lark and Abe ran out to meet him. From their expressions, he figured he must look pretty bad.

"What in the world happened to you over at that mining camp, son?" Abe asked as he helped him to dismount.

"Nothing good. Todd's the one who's behind this robbery scheme. He's the one Mohler's working for. Since he's the mine superintendent, he'll know when that gold is being shipped out and can tip the outlaws off."

"Well, I'll be . . ." said Abe. "It sure fits. Fits like a glove on a hand."

"Come on inside," said Lark. "You need something to eat, and you're chilled to the bone."

He couldn't argue with her there.

Stovall was sitting up on his bunk. He appeared to be feeling stronger even though he looked like he'd been trampled by a herd of buffalo.

"Did you run into Mohler and his outfit, too?" he asked, glancing at the bruise on the side of Shad's face. "You sure look like it."

"Nope. But I did run into his boss over at Last Chance. Have to say we didn't take to each other."

"Are you talking about Todd?"

"Yes. I discovered that he's the one who's calling the shots. Mohler and his bunch are just the hired hands."

"Makes a whole lot of sense," said Stovall. "I've met Todd a time or two and he struck me as being a weasel. Never did trust him."

"When is the gold being shipped out?" asked Abe.

Shad shrugged. "I can't say for sure, but from the way Todd was acting, I'm betting it's soon. Maybe even today."

He sat down on a bench near the fire. Lark draped a blanket over his shoulders and brought him a cup of coffee, steaming hot.

"Thanks," he said. "I spent a lot of time lying on a dirt floor. Thought I was going to freeze before I could get here. Up this high, it gets cold at night."

"Where do you think they'll attack the wagon?" asked Stovall.

Shad turned to Toby. "Did you hear them say anything about that?"

The kid shook his head. "No, but they were going to

hide the wagon somewhere in a barn outside of Cimarron and divide up the gold."

That didn't help much. Shad leaned his back against the wall and took a swallow of coffee. It warmed him all the way down.

"I'm wondering how many men Todd will send along to guard that gold shipment," said Abe.

Shad had been thinking about that too. Todd wouldn't want to let any more in on his scheme than he absolutely had to. He figured Bledsoe was the only one who knew. So chances were the mine superintendent would only send enough guards to avoid arousing suspicion. Bledsoe would undoubtedly be one of them.

"My guess is not many," he answered. "To get that wagon safely down, they're going to have to keep to the trail. I think we'd better ride down there and wait. We'll stay off to the side where we can watch and not be seen. Then when they pass by, we'll follow along at a distance and keep an eye on 'em. When trouble breaks out, we'll join the party."

"Are you sure you're up to this, son?" asked Abe. "You don't look too good."

"I'm fine," said Shad, touching a finger to the bruise on the side of his face. "Though I've probably looked better."

"Well, before we go, I'll fry you up a pan of bacon. Stovall's got some canned peaches too. It won't take me long, and I'll throw in another pot of coffee to boot."

"Oh, I can do that," said Lark, stepping over to the cookstove.

"I'd sure appreciate the help," said Abe.

"I spent most of the night digging out of that shed

they had me locked in," said Shad. "I feel like a gopher and I'm hungry as a bear. Whatever you cook, I'll be glad to eat."

While the two prepared breakfast, Shad went out and saddled the *gruello* that had belonged to Scott. While he was tying his bedroll behind the saddle, Toby joined him.

"Do you think those mine owners will give us a nice reward for getting their gold back?" he asked.

The question irritated him. "Truth is, I've got no idea what they'll do. Aren't you even a little bit worried about your pa?"

Toby turned away. When he looked back, his eyes were misted.

"Shad, I can't even let myself believe that he's sick, let alone dying. There. I said the word 'dying.' "

"Well, you're going to have to believe it, and you're going to have to face up to it, for it's true. I only hope that Nat's still around by the time we get you back to the ranch."

Toby sighed. "It's going to be hard to see him like that. Real sick, I mean. He's always been so strong. Why, he could outwork anybody on the ranch."

What he said was true enough.

"If you weren't so ornery, you'd be home where you're supposed to be, and me and Abe wouldn't have to be chasing you all over the country. Not to mention this mess you've gotten us into with Mohler and Todd."

"Well, I am the way I am," Toby said. "I've got a right to be too."

Shad could sympathize with his need to plot his own course. He'd had his own problems in that regard. He remembered how he'd felt when the Judge had sent him away to St. Louis after his father was murdered. The Judge had insisted that he go to a big city school and then study the law. But he hadn't wanted to leave the place he'd always known, and he'd cared not a stitch for becoming a lawyer. A man needed to choose his own path. He figured that was what Toby was trying to do.

"I can understand," Shad said, scratching the *gruel-lo*'s ears. "We've all got to be who we are and do whatever seems right to us."

The tension eased in Toby's youthful, unlined face. "Well, I'm glad that somebody finally understands me."

When they went back inside, the aroma of bacon filled the small room. Abe handed him a heaping plate of food, and Shad dug in with gusto. When he'd finished eating, he wiped his sleeve across his mouth and got up.

"It's time to get a move on," he said. "Miss Lark, we're leaving Stovall in your good care."

"Just remember who you're dealing with," she said. "I know those men. They'll all be jumpy, and any one of them would kill you without an instant's hesitation."

"If I was guarding that much gold, I'd be jumpy, too," said Stovall. "That yellow stuff invites no-accounts to try to steal it."

Lark stood in the doorway, watching as they rode out of the clearing, their spare mounts on lead ropes.

"That's a fine woman," said Shad. "She'll make somebody a good wife."

"Could be you're right," said Abe. "Could be you're right."

The three of them made their way down the mountainside. They headed toward the trail single-file, always traveling at an angle to the south. When they drew near to it, Shad held up his hand for silence.

"Wait here," he said. "I'll go on down and see if they've already passed by."

He went the rest of the way alone. Except for the sounds of nature, the mountain was quiet. When he reached the trail, he saw that there were no fresh wagon ruts. That was good. It meant they were in time. From the tension he'd sensed in Todd back at Last Chance, he felt that the shipment was due to go out very soon. He made his way back up to the others.

"We're in luck," he reported. "They've not been by yet. Now what we have to do is wait."

Toby looked uncertain. "Why is it you think that the robbery is going to take place anywhere around here?"

"You tell him," said Abe.

"Well, the valley between here and the canyon is wide open. There's no place to hide. You can see for miles. There's a ranch or two in the distance and there's cattle grazing here and there. Then, too, there's oft times a few travelers moving between Taos and Cimarron. Always a chance there could be witnesses. If so, it would mean interference. Or someone to report to the law if they managed to get away.

"Now, it won't happen in the canyon, either, for those guards would spot the outlaws as they crossed the valley. What's more, they wouldn't hesitate to shoot. Todd knows this."

Toby pulled a wry face. "So it'll happen before they get to the valley. That'll make it real soon. Right?"

"That's about the size of it, son," said Abe. "It'd be nice if someone was to ride in here and tell us when, but since that ain't going to happen, we wait."

It turned out that their wait was a short one. Shad heard the lumbering wagon and the sounds of approaching mules and horses in the distance. He signaled the others to move farther back, where they were better screened behind a thick stand of firs. His breathing grew shallow and his heart beat faster as the entourage drew closer.

It didn't take long for the wagon and guards to come into view. It wasn't impressive. Certainly not to anyone who didn't know the nature of the cargo. Bledsoe was driving the wagon. Two well-armed riders led and two more followed close behind. They passed by and went on down the trail. As soon as they were out of sight, around the curve of the mountain, Shad signaled the others to follow.

"We'll stay off to the side, among the trees," he said. "The going will be harder that way, but they won't be able to spot us. Neither will the outlaws."

No sooner had he spoken than a gunshot echoed on the slope. Dirt geysered up in front of the *gruello*. The startled horse reared. It was all Shad could do to keep him under control.

"Get down!" he managed to shout to the others.

Then, following his own advice, he grabbed his rifle from its boot and hit the ground running.

Another shot followed the first. It came so close that he felt the breeze as it tore past his ear. Dropping like a rock, he rolled into the underbrush. There he paused and panted for breath. Somewhere up above them, a killer was hidden. He peered through the brush, trying to spot him. What he saw was a large boulder perched on the mountainside. It was the perfect hiding place for a sniper.

Suddenly, a spate of gunfire sounded in the distance. It was coming from the direction of the gold wagon.

The attack had begun. Instead of riding to the rescue as he'd planned, they were pinned down and helpless. He glanced over and saw that Abe was hunkered down nearby. Toby had taken refuge behind a tree.

"Abe, you and Toby give me some cover-fire," Shad said. "I'm going to try to work my way up that slope."

"Will do," said Abe. "You be careful, now."

Shad moved out, keeping to the underbrush. He crawled off to the side, away from the gunman's direct line of vision. His partners were drawing the sniper's attention and his gunfire. This gave him the chance to work his way up the slope. He was almost to the top when a foothold gave way. He slid downward, all the while clawing desperately for a handhold. At last, he was able to stop himself. His face stung from scraping a sharp rock and his mouth tasted of dirt. He took a deep breath, hoping it wouldn't be his last. Then he hurriedly checked the rifle to make sure it was still in working order. Finding that it was, he started climbing again toward the sniper's stronghold.

It was plain that only one man was shooting at them. The rest must have been needed for the robbery. When Shad reached the top, a boulder blocked his view of the sniper. He slung the rifle over his shoulder and dropped on all fours to crawl around it. The shooter was close now.

Shad had almost cleared the rock barrier when he heard a yelp from below. It sounded like Toby had been hit.

"Shadrach!" called Abe. "I'm afraid they've got us. It's Mohler's man. He heard the shots and doubled back."

"Drop your gun and come down from there!" yelled

a familiar voice, one that he'd heard at the outlaws' campfire.

"Kill 'em if he doesn't!" ordered another familiar voice from beyond the rock barrier. Clay Todd was the sniper. He must have followed the gold shipment to make sure that nothing went wrong.

Shad knew that the only thing keeping his friends alive was the weapon in his hand. There was one other thing in his favor—they didn't know exactly where he was.

From where he was crouched, he could see Abe clearly. Toby, too. The boy was sitting on the ground, cradling his wounded arm. Nearby, the outlaw with the broken nose was holding a gun on them.

"Get on down there, Wakefield," said Todd. "I know you can hear me."

Shad kept silent. He couldn't see Todd, but he had a clear shot at Broken Nose. He brought up the carbine, looked down the sights, and fired. The shot echoed on the mountain. Broken Nose fell where he stood. Abe and Toby scrambled for cover and found it an instant before Todd started shooting again.

Shad motioned for Abe to climb the slope that led to the other side of the boulder. It was his plan that together they'd form a pincer and trap Todd in his stronghold. Now that they were out of sight, and Todd no longer had a clear target, the firing had ceased again. Shad waited until his partner had time to get into place. Then, gun in hand, he moved around the boulder, preparing to attack. To his surprise, the sniper's lair was empty. Todd had fled.

The forest was dense where it hugged the rock spill. It provided cover almost immediately. From somewhere within this wilderness came the sound of a horse blowing through its nostrils. Shad started to run toward it, but he was too late. Retreating hoof beats told the story. Todd was escaping.

"He's getting away!" Shad yelled over to Abe. "He had his horse tied back there. We can't catch him now."

"I heard," said Abe. "We'd better go back down and see about Toby."

By the time they got back to where Toby was waiting, their horses had all returned. The boy was leaning against a tree looking pale and hurt. Abe examined his upper arm. The bullet had grazed the fleshy part and passed on. But the hole it left was bloody. No doubt it hurt like the dickens. The older man fetched a bottle of whiskey from his supplies and poured a liberal amount on the wound. Toby winced.

"It's just a scratch, boy," said Abe. "You were real lucky. It wasn't even your right arm that got hurt."

"Don't worry," said Toby. "I can still shoot."

Shad wondered what the boy's pa would think about his son being mixed up in this business and getting shot. But then at the rate they were going, chances were Nat wouldn't be around to hear about it.

Abe took a bandage and wrapped the whiskey-soaked wound. "That should keep you out of trouble, Tobias," he said.

"Yeah. I reckon it'll do. Thanks."

Shad was anxious to get underway.

"My guess is that Todd won't be far from that wagon. He must have been following along, keeping an eye on things, when he spotted us."

"Are we going to chase after the gold robbers or are we going to dig a grave?" asked Toby.

Shad's first impulse was to leave Broken Nose where

he lay. But then he changed his mind. It was too late to help the guards, anyway.

"All right," he said. "I guess it won't take us long to scoop out a hole and pile some rocks over him. It's the best we can do and more'n he deserves."

He and Abe set about the task while Toby stood guard. As soon as the last rock was piled over the outlaw's final resting place, they mounted up and rode on down the trail.

"Burying that fellow let the outlaws get a big lead on us," said Toby. "Maybe we shouldn't've done it."

Now's a fine time to worry about it, thought Shad.

"They already had a lead on us," he said. "But it won't matter much, I guess. We know where they're going."

"To town?"

"Yep. They're headed for that barn you told us about. I'd bet my saddle on it."

It wasn't long before they reached the spot where the wagon had been attacked. There was no mistaking it. Four bodies lay sprawled on the ground where blood had been spilled. The miners serving as guards had been shot without warning. Shad noticed that Todd's man Bledsoe wasn't among them, not that he'd expected him to be.

"Well, that answers one question," he said. "Todd didn't pay off the guards."

"It's a cryin' shame," said Abe. "Those fellows most likely had themselves families that need 'em."

"More burying?" asked Toby.

"Yes," said Shad.

There was no help for it. They got busy and scooped out a mass grave. Toby pitched in as best he could with his good arm. When it was done, they removed their hats while Abe bowed his head and recited a scripture that he knew from memory. When he was through, Shad put his hat back on and mounted the *gruello*. They rode until darkness forced them to stop and make camp.

They were about to climb into their bedrolls when Toby spoke up.

"Todd knows we're after him, and that we'll chase him clear to purgatory if necessary. Do you think that he or any of the other outlaws are apt to backtrack and try to shoot us while we're asleep?"

Shad had already considered the possibility.

"They might. That's why we're going to take turns keeping watch tonight. I'm volunteering to go first."

While the others slept, he sat alone in the dark, the Spencer at hand. The ache in his head was almost gone now, but his gut and ribs were still sore. Todd's man, Bledsoe, hadn't been gentle. Shad had known other men like Todd. They were minnows who wanted to be whales, men who lusted for money and for power. They wanted fine living and lots of respect, even the envy of others. But they couldn't make anything of themselves, so they stole from the ones who'd succeeded. What none of them seemed to realize was that a man who failed at everything else was apt to fail at robbery, too.

The hours passed uneventfully. When Abe took his place, Shad was ready to bed down. At daylight they ate a meager meal and got underway.

They soon left the mountain behind and entered the sprawling valley. You could see for a long stretch, but there was no sign of the outlaws, nor of the gold wagon.

"They got a bigger lead on us than I expected," said Shad.

"True," said Abe, "but we've pared back their numbers by two outlaws, if you count Scott."

Still, there was Mohler, Bledsoe, and a couple of others. There was also Todd, who'd surely joined them. According to Toby, the man who'd shot him and been killed in return was named Quillen. That left Thurman, the one he'd called Red Beard. It also left the pockmarked Strong. Five men all together—and every last one of them was a killer.

Chapter Eight

After a time, they stopped to give the horses a breather. Shad went to one of the saddlebags and took out a spyglass. With a sharp snap, he opened the sections to their full length and began to scan the area that stretched out before them.

"See anything?" asked Abe.

"No. There's no sign of 'em."

Shad realized they had some catching up to do. The outlaws had been covering the miles. They apparently didn't care how hard they were working the mules or how much harm they were doing to them. Most likely they'd traveled throughout the night. It might be better to confront them elsewhere, anyway, he figured. Here, it would be two men and a wounded kid, out in the open, against five outlaws. Not good odds. To his way of thinking, they'd stand a better chance following them and trapping them in the barn where they planned to stash the wagon and divvy up the gold. It sounded easy. He knew it wouldn't be. Todd was aware they were on his trail and he'd try to stop them—any way he could.

"Since we don't see 'em, they must've gone on through the night," said Abe. "Awful hard on the animals, that's for sure."

No surprise. They'd want to get that wagon under cover before the alarm went out.

"It's all my fault that we fell so far behind," said Toby. "I was the one that wanted those graves dug."

"It was the proper thing to do," said Abe, "and we'd've done it anyway. Don't worry, son, we'll catch up to 'em."

Truth be told, Shad would prefer to have Toby in a safe place when they did. It might have been a mistake not sending the boy back to Colorado on his own. But that would have been risky with the outlaws gunning for him. Then, too, there was Toby's penchant for getting into trouble, along with his reluctance to return home. Shad didn't quite trust his sudden change of mind. He shrugged off the nagging doubts. Worrying about decisions, whether they'd been right or wrong, was a waste of time. Sometimes things happened and nothing you could do was exactly right. You just had to make a choice and do the best you could.

Soon they were underway again. A soft breeze rippled the grass, bringing with it the scent of the pines that grew higher up. This was good grazing land. It made him think of home. There was a lot of work to be done at his ranch. McNary was a good foreman, a man he'd trusted with his life more than once. On the other hand, leaving things to somebody else wasn't the same as being there. Still, he owed a debt to Nat Granger for pulling him away from that bull's horns. The least he could do was fetch his boy home. Anyway, that was what he'd thought when he'd started. But he hadn't bargained on getting beaten up and shot at by gold thieves. It seemed that life dealt hands like this sometimes. All a man could do was take the cards and play them the best he knew how. He'd done that after his friend Charlie had been murdered by a land-grabbing outlaw, and again when that overbearing Craddock woman had nearly gotten him killed. But it was at times like these that he longed for a peaceful life.

His old friend must have sensed his thoughts. "Shadrach, whatever else has gone wrong, we're headed toward home."

"Maybe we're going in the right direction," he agreed, "but I wouldn't say we're exactly close by."

"Trying to make you feel better, that's all."

"Thanks for trying, but it didn't work."

Toby, who'd been trailing a little behind, rode up to them.

"Do you think anyone back there at that mining camp is wise to Todd?" he asked.

"I doubt it," said Shad. "I don't think he'd risk leaving anyone in Last Chance who might tip off the mine owners."

Abe glanced over their back trail. "Uh-oh. Somebody's hightailing it this way."

Shad turned in the saddle and squinted into the distance. He could make out two horses. One was on a lead line. The other was a blood bay. The rider was Larkspur Russell. Abe recognized her, too.

"Now what in tarnation . . ." he started.

"Why, it's Miss Lark," Toby blurted out. "What's she doing here? She's supposed to be back on the mountain looking after Davie."

"Reckon it won't be long before you can ask her to her face," said Abe. "Sure wish she'd stayed where she belonged."

Shad agreed. He begrudged the time they were wasting, waiting for her to catch up. Other than Toby, Larkspur Russell was the last person he wanted around when the showdown with the outlaws came. He noticed the grim expression on Abe's face and wondered what his friend would say to the woman he so obviously admired.

When she finally rode up and swung down from the saddle, her face was flushed. Before anyone could say anything, she started talking fast. "Now don't go getting mad at me. I had to come along."

"What about Stovall?" said Shad. "Considering the condition he's in, I don't think it was wise to go off and leave him back there by himself."

She fixed him with her wide blue eyes.

"Cornelius, the hermit, came wandering in not long after you rode out. He was worried about Toby. When he saw what the outlaws had done to Davie, he agreed to stay on while I went after you. I think Cornelius misses Toby. Fact is, I think he's starting to get lonesome staying up there all by himself. Anyway, you needn't fret. Davie's in good hands."

That the Mad Hatter had suddenly become sociable surprised Shad. But then he'd known stranger things to happen. Maybe Toby had succeeded in calling him back from whatever dark corner of his soul he'd crawled into. It could be that Cornelius was ready at last to join the world again.

He could see that Abe was struggling to hold his temper and was on the verge of losing the battle.

"Lark Russell, this is no place for you to be," he protested. "We're on the trail of a pack of killers. Since we left Stovall's place, we've already been ambushed. Toby here got shot, and they outright murdered four of the miners that Todd sent along to guard the wagons. They was doomed from the minute they set foot out of Last Chance."

It was plain by the look on her face that she was shocked by the news. Still, she appeared determined.

"Abe Featherstone, I'm not going to let you, Shad, and Toby go up against those criminals alone. I promise you I can shoot as straight as anyone. When the chips are down, I won't cut and run."

She was a strong, hardheaded woman. Shad couldn't help but admire her grit.

"Besides, there's something you don't know," she went on. "Davie is more than just a friend of my father. He's my father's cousin. Blood kin, if that means anything. What's more, I owe him a lot. He helped me when I was first starting out. On top of that, he kept my secret about being a woman. That worthless pack of coyotes rode in there and beat the poor man half to death for no reason. It makes me sick, and it makes me mad. I intend to be there when you catch up with them."

Abe sighed and looked resigned. It appeared to Shad that Miss Lark Russell had won the first round.

"Son, is it all right with you?" Abe asked.

He shrugged. "You can't stop a prairie cyclone. There's no point in trying."

"Good," said Lark, a note of triumph in her voice. "Now, it's time I changed horses."

Abe glanced over at the fine-looking strawberry mare.

"Where'd you get that horse?" he asked as she went about the business of switching the saddle.

"I borrowed him."

"You don't say. Well, in this part of the country, they hang a fellow for 'borrowing' like that."

She shot him a look that said, "don't be ridiculous."

"I borrowed him from Cornelius. He was kind enough to lend Strawberry to me. Figured I'd need a spare."

Abe scowled. "You're getting mighty chummy with a fellow that you only saw one time before."

As Shad listened to the exchange, it appeared to him that Abe was starting to stake a claim on the woman. What was more, she was enjoying his reaction.

"I have to confess that I was surprised at how friendly and helpful he was," she said. "Cornelius will be good company for Davie."

"Were you dressed up like a man and talking in that raspy voice of yours?"

She smiled at him. "As a matter of fact, I wasn't. Davie explained my situation and Cornelius said he thought I had spunk."

Except for the fact that she was wearing trousers and riding astride her horse like a man, she still wasn't disguised. Lark was a handsome woman. No denying that. But she certainly was an unusual one. Shad noticed the rifle in her saddle scabbard and the pistol that was stuck in her belt. Miss Lark was full of surprises.

"Well, let's get on with it," said Abe, ignoring Toby's smirk. "We're standing here burning daylight."

They rode eastward until they could see the slope that led up to the head of the high canyon. Shad halted. The place looked the same as when they'd ridden down it a matter of days before. Still, for anyone approaching from the west, it could prove dangerous.

"Is something wrong?" asked Toby.

"Maybe. It occurred to me they might leave someone behind. Post him up there to wait and pick us off. It's the way I'd do it in their place."

"What is it you've got in mind?" said Abe, looking at him expectantly.

"Precaution."

Again, he snapped open the spyglass and scanned the slope, as well as the area around it. When he came to a thick growth of scrub at the top, he paused and focused on it. A perfect hiding place for a sniper. Its color was dusty green, except for one small patch of blue. Not the blue of any wildflower, but the color of cloth.

"Somebody's up there," Shad said.

Toby turned pale. "If I'd been by myself, I'd've ridden right into his gunsights."

"I'll get my rifle and have a go at him," said Abe.

"No, wait," Shad ordered. "Leave him to me. I'll need to get closer, though. See if you can distract him. Get off your horses and walk around. Look like you're going to make camp—anything."

"We'll give 'er a try," said Abe. "Now, don't go getting yourself shot."

They busied themselves out of range of the sniper, while Shad rode slowly off to the left at an angle. He, too, was visible to the gunman at the top of the slope but, little by little, he worked himself closer, pretending to look for fuel. At last, he came within range. He brought up the Spencer to get off a shot, but the gunman spotted his action and raised up and fired. The bullet was off the mark, but not by much. Shad sighted in on him and squeezed the trigger. The blue color disappeared.

He prodded the dun and took off. The big horse cat-hopped up the slope to where the outlaw had been stationed. No one was there. Gun in hand, Shad slid from the saddle and inspected the ground where the sniper had crouched and waited. Near the scrub were a couple of piñon trees that provided some shade. Beneath them were the remains of half a dozen cigarettes, along with an empty whiskey bottle. There was also a puddle of blood. Farther back, he found fresh horse droppings. The outlaw had been hit badly enough to bleed, but he wasn't dead. He'd headed down the canyon, and in the canyon there were countless places to hide.

The others had been watching, and they came riding up.

"Did you see who it was?" said Abe.

"Only caught a glimpse. I think it was Strong." He pointed to the blood. "I hit him."

"Looks like," his friend concurred.

"Do you think he'll go on ahead and try to bushwhack us again?" asked Lark.

Shad shook his head.

"No, not with him being hurt like that. I'm betting he won't stick around. Still, we'd best keep alert."

All except Lark switched mounts. Then they entered the canyon. By the time they reached the place where they'd encountered Scott, Lark's expression was plenty grim. Shad couldn't guess what was going through her mind. Nothing pleasant, for sure. But whether she liked it or not, they'd be spending another night close by.

At dusk, he suggested they stop and make camp. "Up on the flank," he said. "I'd feel safer there."

The others agreed. They left the canyon floor and climbed higher on the slope. Here they made their camp among the pines. Abe did the cooking in spite of Lark's protests.

While they were filling their plates at the fire, Shad heard a noise in the underbrush. Taking care not to attract attention, he shifted his plate to his left hand and started to reach for his pistol grips with the other.

"I wouldn't do that if I was you," came a warning from the dark. "All of you keep your hands in sight."

This was a new voice. One he didn't recognize. He'd been afraid that Strong had doubled back to kill them. But had Strong managed to sneak up on them, they'd most likely be dead. The outlaw wasn't the kind to give a fellow notice.

"Who are you?" he asked. "What do you want?"

"I suspect the same thing that you want. You're the one that dug the hole under the shed back at Last Chance, I take it."

Shad decided he must be one of the miners.

"I dug it," he admitted. "Todd had his henchman beat me up and lock me in there until he could come back later and kill me. He figured that I knew too much about his plans to rob the gold shipment."

"I'm not at all surprised. The Kinion boy told me about you. How you'd ridden into town wanting to talk to the mine supervisor. Then how Bledsoe carried you out and dumped you into that shed. I never did trust Todd, the way he talks, the way he acts. He's a rattlesnake, for sure."

"If we're on the same side," said Shad, "then maybe you'd better come on in and introduce yourself. Have something to eat and some hot coffee."

"Obliged. Don't mind if I do. I've been in the saddle too long today."

While Shad watched, a rangy fellow with long, tied-back hair climbed off his horse and walked into the circle of firelight.

"Name's Ross Lurvey," he said. "I represent the mine owners' interests. Supposed to be a messenger, but I keep my eye on things, as well.

"When I last saw Todd, I had a feeling that he was up to something. He was nervous as a cat with its tail under a rocker when I turned up at Last Chance."

"What happened?" asked Lark.

"I decided to worry him a little. Let him know that the mine owners were suspicious and on guard in the form of myself. But I couldn't stick around. I was in a hurry to get to Elizabethtown, or E-town as some call it. Had business there. When I got back, the gold shipment had gone out. But so had Todd. His housekeeper was worried about him, the way he took off. Appears she has a soft spot for him."

Shad introduced himself and the others, and Lark filled Lurvey's plate. He found himself a seat on the ground and dug in like he was half starved.

"Saw the graves," he said between bites. "Those poor fellows didn't stand a chance. Todd marked 'em for death the minute he picked 'em out."

"We followed along," said Shad. "Thought maybe we could even the odds a little, but Todd bushwhacked us. Quillen heard the gunshots and came back to help him. Got in front of a bullet, himself, and died of lead poisoning."

"I'm surprised you'd bring a woman along," said

Lurvey, discreetly glancing at Lark in the firelight. She glared at him in return.

"We didn't," said Abe. "She brung herself. Followed us. It's a good thing she wasn't along when we had that set-to with Todd and that other outlaw."

Lark had a determined set to her jaw.

"I've got my reasons for being here," she said. "Don't worry about me. I promise I won't be a burden."

"She did manage to get here in time for our run-in with Strong," said Shad. "He was waiting for us at the canyon."

"I noticed. Looks like you got some lead into him. I saw the blood."

"Did your bosses really suspect Todd would do something like this?"

Lurvey shifted his weight and reached for the coffee pot to refill his cup.

"I've got to tell you, they're not a trusting group of men. Blair, Brownsworth, and Hale aren't about to put their blind trust in anybody. They're fully aware that gold can corrupt the most upright of men, which I don't believe Todd ever was in the first place. To check on him was my job. I'd ride in from time to time and look things over. Mostly use my instincts. Then report back to them."

"So it would seem that you've got a big stake in finding these outlaws, too, Mr. Lurvey," said Lark.

"You might say that. My reputation is on the line and my reputation means a lot to me. Got any ideas where they might be headed?"

Toby glanced over at Shad. He nodded his assent. "Go ahead and tell him."

"I kinda got mixed up with 'em for a while," the boy admitted. "When I wanted to leave, they wouldn't let me. Figured they'd get some ransom money from my pa to let me go. Anyway, I heard 'em talking about their plan to rob the gold shipment. They mentioned where they'd stash the wagon 'til they could get it divvied up."

Lurvey was giving him his full attention. "And where might that be?" he asked.

"They said there was a barn this side of Cimarron. The place is pretty much abandoned. They were going to pull the wagon inside."

Lurvey leaned his back against a tree. In the firelight, his expression was thoughtful.

"It appears we've got 'em, then. It's only a matter of trapping them in that barn before they divide the gold and take off in different directions."

Shad didn't care for the way Lurvey assumed the job would be easy.

"Remember," he warned, "there's five of 'em. That is, if Strong gets back and he's not hurt too bad. Bledsoe is in on this, too. And they've all got a lot to lose."

"Bledsoe!" Lurvey spat. "Todd's lapdog. The fellow hasn't got a brain in his head. I sure can't see Todd forking over a fifth of that gold to someone like him. You might say that Bledsoe is highly dispensable."

On that point, Shad agreed. "I don't imagine his life expectancy will be too long once Todd doesn't have any more use for him."

"I've never cared much for the Last Chance mine supervisor, either," said Lark, "and the more I hear, the more I detest him."

Lurvey set his empty plate down beside him. "I

expect you've got a lot of company there, ma'am. He's not made a lot of friends."

"We'll be glad to have you with us," said Shad. "If you intend to ride along, we leave at first light."

The newcomer chuckled. "Wouldn't have it any other way."

While they bedded down, Lurvey went off a ways by himself and spread out his blankets. He appeared to be a loner, a man who needed a lot of his own company. Maybe not as much as Cornelius, but more than most.

At first light, they made do with hot coffee and warmed-over pan bread before they broke camp. Farther on, they found the remains of a fire and a dis-carded bloody bandage.

"Strong appears to be hanging on," Lurvey observed.

That he was still alive meant he'd be reporting to Todd soon. The outlaws would know that he'd failed to pick them off. They'd also learn that Shad and the oth-ers were still on their trail.

The morning slipped away. In the mountains behind them, dark clouds had formed around the peaks. Shad looked back at just the right moment to see forked lightning shoot out from one of them. Its power was awesome. Less than an hour passed before thunder began to rumble across the sky. The storm was swiftly moving toward them. He could smell it now. They stopped to don their slickers and were none too soon. The sky opened and began to pour buckets.

"This gully-washer is going to wipe out all of Strong's tracks," said Lurvey, shouting to be heard over the driving rain.

"Doesn't matter," said Shad. "I know where he's going."

"I'm trusting you to be right, Wakefield."

Shad was trusting Toby and the outlaws' loose talk. But common sense told him they would have to get that gold wagon out of sight somewhere. As he recalled, the barn would be the first place they'd come to that was suitable. If nobody had known of the robbery, it would have been the perfect hiding place. They'd planned to be long gone by the time the theft was discovered. At least Todd had planned to be long gone.

Toby rode with his hat brim pulled low over his face and his slicker wrapped tight around him. If his wounded arm bothered him, he was keeping it to himself. It was a small sign of maturity. Lark rode close beside Abe. Shad figured that neither one of them minded the rain too much. Lurvey appeared to be watching everywhere. He intended for nothing to surprise him.

Outside the canyon, where it was relatively flat, there was no shelter. They had no choice but to ride out the storm. Fortunately, at this time of year rainstorms usually didn't last long. As a rule, the heavens opened, it poured for awhile, and then it stopped. But while the downpour did last, it slowed them up.

The soil was quickly turned into a loblolly that they had to slog through. It was hard for Shad to imagine how quickly it would dry once the sun came out. The arid ground was always thirsty, and what moisture it couldn't drink would quickly evaporate or else run into arroyos. Several minutes passed before the rain ceased abruptly. In the storm's wake, everything smelled fresh and clean.

"It's my guess that we'll be close to the barn by nightfall," said Shad.

"Good enough," said Lurvey. "Lead the way. I'm right behind you."

After the late September sun had sunk below the horizon, the darkened sky was cloudless. A thousand stars appeared with nothing at all to obscure them. On top of that, a full moon draped its soft light over the Northern New Mexico landscape. At another time Shad would have welcomed it, but not on this night.

Abe, too, saw the problem.

"Them owlhoots will be able to spot us riding up to 'em, plain as day," he said. "We won't stand the chance of a pie at a picnic."

What he said was true and it was worrisome. At last, Shad could see the silhouette of the barn. It lay some distance off to the side of the trail. Tonight it was bathed in muted moonlight. On their way west, he recalled seeing it and also the abandoned house that stood nearby. Even from afar he could tell that the house had fallen into ruin. But the barn had appeared to be in much better shape.

"Abe, we'll leave the horses here with Lark and Toby," he said. "You and Lurvey come with me."

He slung the carbine over his shoulder and checked the pearl-handled pistol. The confiscated gun was fancy, but he much preferred his own, the one that Todd had taken from him back at Last Chance.

"We'll move in low," he directed. "We'd better cover the distance slow at first. That way they might not notice. It's movement they're apt to spot. Keep to the shadows if you can find any. Don't start shooting unless they do."

"You're the boss," said Abe.

Shad noticed that Lurvey didn't second the part about his being the boss. It was plain the mine owners' agent was making his own decisions and answering to no one. This was all right with him. He gave the signal to advance.

They spread out, and crouching low, they sprinted short distances at a time. When they got up close, they crawled. The mud had already dried and so had the grass. For this he was thankful. If the outlaws had left a guard, Shad wasn't able to spot him. He figured the horses must be inside, too. At the door they paused to listen. Nothing. Not a sound. The wooden bar that fastened it was hanging loose. This probably meant that someone was inside. The others noticed it too.

While they covered him, Shad yanked the door open. Gun drawn, he threw himself inside and landed belly-down on the floor. It was a good thing, for bullets flew over his head. He hoped that Abe and Lurvey weren't standing in the doorway. The gunfire was coming from the loft. Shad rolled over and aimed the pistol upward, toward where the last shot had originated. He squeezed the trigger.

There was a cry of pain. The firing ceased.

Lurvey and Abe slipped inside the barn.

"You hurt, Shadrach?" his partner asked.

"No. Stay back. He's up there. It might be a trap."

Silently, carefully, Shad inched his way over to the ladder that was made barely visible by the moonlight from the doorway. Meanwhile, Abe was making some noise on the other side of the barn. If the shooter was still alive and able to fire a gun, that noise might serve as a distraction.

By feel, Shad climbed the ladder one rung at a time.

As his head came up above the level of the loft, he steeled himself, knowing he might catch a bullet or the toe of a boot. There was neither and he pulled himself onto solid flooring. Here there was the smell of hay mixed with gun smoke.

It was dark but he could hear the raspy breathing of the man who'd tried to kill him. He was only a few yards away. For sure, he wasn't dead. Just as sure, he was armed. This called for continued stealth. Silently he crawled across the hay until he reached the prone sniper. Most likely, the gun would be in his right hand. It was. Shad tucked it safely in his belt.

"Wasn't worth it," mumbled the dying man in front of him. "Wasn't worth the thirty dollars he paid me to kill anybody who came nosing around here."

"Do you mean Todd?" Shad asked.

"Didn't tell me his name. Uppity fellow. Acted like he was better'n everybody."

"That was Todd. Where is he now? Where is that gold shipment he was going to hide in here?"

"Don't know. I never saw any gold. I rode out from Cimarron. Was supposed to wait in this barn. It was his man, Mohler, who hired me. Then Uppity comes prancing in here. I looked out and saw a wagon and more men in the distance, but they never left the trail. He comes in here and gives me thirty dollars. Then he tells me to shoot anybody who comes nosing around. That's all I can tell you."

It was, for sure, all that he was ever going to tell. He took a spell of coughing. Then he died.

"Did you hear that?" Shad called to the others.

"Most of it," said Abe.

Shad made his way back down the ladder and struck

a match. By its light, he located a lantern that hung nearby. In the lantern light, they searched the place from one end to the other. Aside from one bedraggled horse, no animals had been inside for a long time. The man in the loft had been telling the truth.

"I think Todd never planned to hide the wagon here and split the gold," said Shad. "He had Mohler hire this fellow and Mohler thought he was to guard the place, keep anyone from snooping around. It gave a ring of truth to Todd's story about stopping and splitting the gold equally. I think what he was really going to do was pull the wagon in here, find himself some cover and shoot them before they knew what was happening. With all of them dead, he was free to go his own way with the whole shipment."

"It fits," said Abe. "Then when Toby overheard the outlaws, Todd abandoned the part about stopping off here and getting rid of Mohler and his bunch. Time would be short and there would be bodies to get rid of."

"That's right. I think he took the gold to the place he intended to take it all along, only he had to bring the outlaws, as well."

"Where do you suppose that place is?" asked Abe.

"Good question," said Lurvey. "It's got me buf-faloed. Have you got an answer for that, Wakefield?"

Shad tried to think like Todd. What options did he have?

"Let's go on into town," he said. "Maybe somebody saw them. If not, we can at least get warm and dry. Maybe round up something to eat. Besides, we ought to have the local law send someone out here for the body. The dead man might have kin somewhere close by."

When they got back to where Toby and Lark were

waiting with the horses, Shad had to tell the story all over again.

"So it's on to Cimarron," said Lark.

"Yes, it's on to Cimarron."

Chapter Nine

The hour was late when Shad and his companions rode into Cimarron. Even so, the town was a long way from shutting down for the night. In places, the evening was just beginning. Light and noise spilled from the saloons. There were also lights in the hotel, the cafe, and the jail.

"I expect we'd better stop over at that hotel," said Abe. "See if they have any rooms left to rent."

They tied the horses to the hitch rail and entered the lobby of the National Hotel. Maybe it wouldn't rival the best in St. Louis, Shad thought, but it wasn't bad. The lobby was well lit by kerosene lamps, fancy ones with glass lions' heads on them. It was empty except for the desk clerk, a skinny young fellow with a pencil-thin mustache. He'd loosened his string tie and looked more than half asleep when Shad walked up and rang the bell on the reception desk. He jumped like he'd been shot.

"What can I do for you gentleman and, er . . . lady?"

he asked, looking over their trail-soiled appearances and Lark's masculine clothing with distaste.

"We'd like rooms. One apiece."

The clerk gave the impression of looking down his aquiline nose. "They're quite expensive," he informed them. "Two dollars each. Bath is extra. That is, if you care for such an amenity."

"Fine," said Shad. "We'll take them. Along with the amenity." He reached into his pocket and pulled out a wad of cash.

The desk clerk looked surprised.

"I'll take care of mine," said Lurvey, slapping down a gold piece. "Along with the amenity."

"Same here," said Lark.

They were directed to rooms upstairs. Shad opened the door to his own and lit the lamp. He took it in at a glance. Bed, washstand, pitcher, straight-back chair, lace curtains at the window. Not bad. Certainly better than sleeping in a loft at the livery stable, or wrapped up in blankets on the ground.

A couple of young hired girls brought water for his bath. As soon as they were gone, he pulled off his dirty clothes, climbed in, and washed the accumulation of dust and dirt from his body. When he was done, he wanted nothing more than to pile down on the bed and go to sleep. But rest would have to wait. He got dressed in clean clothes from one of his saddle bags, strapped on the pear-handled pistol, and went downstairs. Abe and the others had already gathered in the lobby and were waiting for him. From his perch behind the reception desk, the night clerk eyed them with suspicion.

"Now that you're here," said Lurvey, "I'm going to

have a look around town. Ask a few questions. See if I can find out anything."

"I already took a look at the hotel register," said Abe. "Fellow over there was kind enough to let me." The clerk glared at him. "None of 'em came in here, not even using bogus names. What names were in the book could be accounted for."

No surprise. Shad hadn't expected them to waltz into the best hotel in town and sign the register. Well, maybe Todd might, he allowed. He appeared to be the kind who liked his creature comforts. Maybe in a weak moment he would've been tempted. Still, there was a lot at stake, far too much to risk for a night in a soft bed. More than likely he'd stick with the others. At least if he was smart, that was what he'd done.

"Well, I don't know about the rest of you," said Lark, "but I'm going out there and find a place to eat. When I'm finished, I'm coming back here and going straight to bed."

"You'd better go along with her, Abe," said Shad. "There's something that I've got to do."

"I'll take the horses over to the livery stable," said Toby. "There's no place around here that you can't walk to, and a little walking will be good for you. It'll stretch your legs."

Lurvey chuckled. "All right, you win. I guess my legs could do with a little stretching."

They separated in front of the hotel. Shad went to the St. John's Bar. It was a different establishment from the one he and Abe had visited on their way west. The saloon was filled with men of various sorts, and a few women who were dressed in gaudy-colored gowns that were a little on the skimpy side. A faro game was in progress at one end. At the other, a fellow with a gold ring on his pinky finger was tinkling the ivories. Shad recognized the tune as one of Stephen Foster's. He approached the bar and ordered a drink. While it was being poured, he asked the aproned barkeep if he'd seen anyone fitting the outlaws' descriptions.

He shook his head. "Nope. Can't say that I recall any of them coming in here."

"One of 'em was wounded. Do you have a doctor in town?"

"Sure do. Doc Tomlin's his name. He's got an office down at the end of the street. Most likely, though, he's at home by now."

"Where's that?"

"Turn right at the bank. Go down about three houses. His name's on the gate."

"Thanks. You got anything to eat here?"

"Bowl of stew. Bowl of beans. Bread that was baked this morning."

"I'll have a bowl of that stew and a slab of bread."

"Fine. Have a chair over there and I'll have Lola bring it to you."

He took his drink and sat down at the table, the only vacant one in the place. From there, he could see the whole room. There was no one that he recognized. His empty stomach complained loudly, but he didn't have to wait long before a buxom woman in a bright green dress approached, bringing food. When he paid her for it, he noticed how the low-cut gown failed to cover a good deal of her flesh. Although he guessed her to be about the same age as Lark, her face was lined and toughened by the circumstances of her life. She smiled at him, a pasted smile that she gave to every man. He added a silver coin for her, which she quickly scooped up.

The stew smelled good, and he dug in with pleasure. As soon as he finished, he pushed back his chair and left the St. Johns. The moon shed plenty of light for him to see by as he made his way over to Doc Tomlin's house. The name was on the gate, just like the barkeep had told him. He struck a match and checked to make sure. Inside the house, a lamp glowed in the window. The doctor hadn't yet retired for the evening. He stepped up and knocked lightly on the door.

A young man, not much older than himself, opened it.

"Yes, what can I do for you?" he asked, squinting into the darkness.

"Dr. Tomlin?"

"I'm Dr. Tomlin."

"I'm here in Cimarron looking for five outlaws that robbed the gold shipment out of Last Chance and killed four guards. I know they were headed this way, for I've been trailing them. Needless to say, they're dangerous. I put a bullet into one of 'em and I thought he might have come by your office for medical treatment."

He gave the doctor descriptions of Todd, Bledsoe, Mohler, and the two other outlaws.

Tomlin shook his head. "No. No wounded man came in for treatment." He hesitated. "Wait. Someone did come in asking to buy laudanum. Said he was out of it and wanted to keep some on hand in case it was needed."

Laudanum killed pain. Maybe the pain of a bullet wound.

"What did the fellow look like?"

"Hard to say. He wore a slicker and his hat was

pulled low. Only thing I can tell you is he had a red beard."

"Thanks, Doc. You've been a big help."

The doctor looked skeptical about that. "Glad you think so," he said.

Shad hurried back to the hotel and took the stairs two at a time. He rapped on Abe's door. There was no answer. Likely he was still out having dinner with Lark. Next he tried Lurvey's room.

The door opened cautiously. "What'd you find out?" Lurvey asked when he saw who it was.

"I think I'm on to something."

"Come in and tell me about it."

Shad stepped inside a room that was a replica of his own.

"I learned that the red-bearded Thurman went to the local doctor's place to buy laudanum," he said. "My guess is Strong was hit pretty bad."

Lurvey nodded. "Sounds like it to me. That doctor didn't happen to notice where Thurman was going, did he?"

"No. It was raining at the time, or else it had just quit, for he was covered up in a slicker. They must have been holed up someplace here in town, though."

"But where? Where in a town this size do you hide a team of mules and a wagon loaded with gold?"

Lurvey's frustration was evident. He was going to have to face the mine owners and tell them how Todd had gotten away with their fortune. Shad didn't envy him the task. He knew that one of the owners, Rossman Blair, was a man with a reputation for ruthlessness.

"I'm stumped," he admitted. "Maybe they left town right after they got the pain medicine for Strong.

Except for Thurman, the rest might not have come into town at all. I'm going to ride out toward the east in the morning and have a look. While the rain may have washed out their tracks for a ways, it didn't last that long. I should be able to pick them up a little farther out. That is, if they went that way."

"I'd like to ride along, if you don't mind."

"Don't mind at all. Be glad of the company."

It wasn't quite daylight when Shad rolled out of bed and jammed his feet into his boots. Next, he strapped on his gun. As he was leaving the room, he ran into Lurvey.

"Good, I see you're ready to ride," he said.

"Are the others going along?"

"No. I think Toby should pay a visit to that sawbones and have him take a look at his arm. Get it fixed up right. I told him so last night."

Abe's door opened. "What's all the racket about?" he asked. "You going off someplace without letting me know?"

"Just for a ride to look for wagon tracks. Thought maybe you ought to stay behind and haul Toby over to that doctor. Let him take a look at that scratch on his arm, and see if you can keep Lark out of trouble while you're at it."

Abe chuckled. "You're giving me the hard jobs, I see."

He had a point.

They collected their horses at the livery stable and Shad rode out on Squire. The town was quiet at this early hour. Nothing was stirring except a stray dog that was sniffing around the café. They rode eastward toward the rising sun. They covered a considerable distance, but the fresh wagon tracks they were looking for simply weren't to be found.

"We should've spotted them by now," said Lurvey. "Right after the rain stopped, they'd have been rolling through mud, leaving a trail that a blind man could follow."

Shad had to admit this was true. And if they'd turned off, it would have been easy to tell. They must have turned south back at Cimarron. If not, they had to be holed up somewhere in town.

"That wagon appears to have dropped off the face of the Earth," said Lurvey.

"Oh, it's still on the Earth. So is Red Thurman, and a bottle of laudanum."

When they got back to town, Toby was waiting for them in the hotel lobby. He was wearing a fresh, professionally applied bandage. Lark and Abe were with him. The night clerk had been replaced by an older man who was polite and acted like he appreciated the fact they'd rented rooms at his establishment.

"I'm ready for some breakfast," said Toby. Shad was ready, too.

They all went to a nearby café, the same one the dog had been sniffing around earlier. The place was filling up fast. He noticed that it was a cut above the ordinary. It sported ruffled curtains, tablecloths, and china plates. He glanced around and recognized one of the diners right off. It was the paunchy barkeep called Schultz. Across from him sat a handsome woman who clearly had expensive taste. She was younger than Schultz by at least a decade, and she wore a ring that had set somebody back a good deal of money. Lark appeared to notice his interest, but didn't say anything.

"Shadrach, when are we going to report that body to the local law?" asked Abe.

"I'm planning to do it right after breakfast. It's been a long morning. Besides, he's not going anywhere."

After they'd eaten and were back outside, Lark asked him what he thought.

"About what?"

"About Inez Schultz. She certainly got your attention."

Shad felt his face redden.

"So that's her name," he said.

"Yes. I've been driving through Cimarron long enough to know. She's Mrs. Bertram Schultz, wife of that bartender."

"She seems a little flashy and 'big city' for a local barkeep's wife," he said as they strolled back toward the hotel.

"I thought so too. But somehow he manages to keep her happy. They have one of the nicest houses in town. Way out past the edge of Cimarron, actually. She has a new plum-colored phaeton and a pair of fine horses. As you probably noticed, she doesn't do too badly when it comes to clothes and jewelry, either."

"That barkeep must have himself another job on the side to be able to spend that kind of money on her."

Lark lifted an eyebrow.

"Well, I wouldn't be surprised," she said. "Either that, or he's running up a lot of debts. But then I guess that's his business and not mine."

Lurvey spoke up. "Why don't I tell the marshal about that body in the barn, 'cause afterward I want to ride back there and snoop around some more. Search his pockets. Have a closer look at the place in the daylight. Could be I'll find something we overlooked. If anybody knows who he is, I want to talk to his friends and family. They might know something. Might find another lead to follow."

"Fine with me," said Shad. "I'm going to hang around town and look some more. Maybe talk to a few people."

They split up at the livery stable, where Lurvey rented a fresh horse. Then, with a wave of his hand, he headed for the jail to report.

"Shadrach, do you want us to tag along with you?" asked Abe.

"No. I think I'll do better if I go alone."

Leaving his friends to their own devices, he mounted up and rode down the main street of town. It was bustling now. When he passed by the café, he noticed Schultz and his wife coming out after finishing their breakfast. To his discomfort, Inez Schultz unabashedly stared at him. Her look was one of admiration and challenge. Not knowing what else to do, he tipped his hat and rode on.

Doctor Tomlin was climbing into his buggy when Shad rode up. He paused and said, "Good morning."

Shad agreed that it was.

"Did you find that wounded outlaw you were looking for?" the doctor asked.

"Nope. Seems like him and his partners have up and disappeared. And they took along all that gold, a wagon, and a team of mules."

Tomlin looked puzzled. "Strange," he said. "They must have left some sort of trail to be followed."

"You'd think. But there's not any sign of 'em. They didn't turn off before they got here and they didn't head east. Lurvey is going to backtrack to that barn and have another look around the place."

"He your partner?"

Shad shook his head. "No, not exactly. He works for the mine owners. I'm just an interested party. A very interested party."

"Sounds like you think they're hiding someplace here in town."

"That's right next door to impossible, isn't it?"

Tomlin shrugged. "I can only pass along a piece of advice a colleague once gave me. After you've exhausted all of the possible answers, then it's time to take a closer look at the impossible ones."

"I'm willing. Maybe you can help."

"Be glad to if I can."

"Where in this town could a person hide a wagon and a team of mules?"

The doctor thought a minute before answering. "Well, of course the livery stable comes to mind first. But I imagine you've already looked there. Then there's a warehouse behind the mercantile that's used by the storekeeper, as well as by a few local businessmen who need storage space from time to time. Other than that, there are quite a few private stables and carriage houses scattered about. Maybe the latter would be a tight squeeze for mules and a wagon, but they could always separate the animals and keep them in a different place."

What he said made sense. "Thanks, Doctor. Appreciate your help."

"Don't mention it."

As Tomlin's buggy pulled away, it occurred to him that there was a carriage house behind the doctor's residence. When Tomlin was out of sight, he went to have a look, ignoring the threatening snarls of a neighbor's dog. The door was wide open and the place was empty. At least it was empty of mules and wagons. He'd already seen the livery stable. So the next most likely place, because of its size, was the warehouse.

Shad made his way to the alley behind the mercantile where the big, shabby warehouse sat. The alley was empty. No one was apt to challenge him. He slid out of the saddle and tried the door. Finding it locked, he walked around the building. At the back, there was a window. At least it had been a window at one time. Someone had nailed weathered boards across the opening to prevent anyone from breaking in. He took a look through the crack between the boards. It was dim inside, but he could see well enough to tell that the interior was absent of mules. It was also absent of a freight wagon of gold.

"Find what it is you're looking for?" came a stern voice from behind him.

He turned, careful to keep his hands in the air away from his gun. The man he faced was big and muscled like a prize fighter. He wore a badge on his shirt and held a six-shooter in his hand.

"As a matter of fact, I didn't, Marshal. It is Marshal, I take it?"

"City marshal. Glover's the name. I just spoke to your friend Lurvey. Sent one of my deputies with him to fetch home that body from the Longley barn. I hear you've been asking questions around town."

"I'm hunting for gold thieves and killers, that's all."

The marshal didn't look pleased.

"I've only got your word for that—and Lurvey's. You might be killers and thieves yourselves, for all I know."

Shad decided to try a different approach. "You've

heard of Rossman Blair and his partners, Brownsworth and Hale, I take it?"

Glover's look was guarded. "I've heard of 'em. What of it?"

"Well, in case Lurvey didn't tell you, it was their gold that was stolen. The one who planned it all and hired the outlaws is Clay Todd, their mine supervisor. Lurvey works for Blair and his partners."

"I see," said Glover. "What's your interest in it?"

"You might say I don't like thieves and killers. But more than that, the outlaws held my young friend prisoner in an attempt to collect ransom. You can add to that the fact that they beat up a helpless old man. Then Todd had his flunky knock me around and kick me in the head. Afterward, he locked me in a shed to be disposed of at a later time. I think you can see that I've got plenty of interest in finding these rattlesnakes."

The marshal appeared to make up his mind. He lowered the gun.

"All right, go on about your business. But I'm warning you to stay out of trouble, not that I expect you will."

"Thank you," Shad said, and lowered his hands.

After the warehouse came up empty, there was nothing left but some stables and carriage houses. He couldn't go searching from place to place all over town. Especially not under Glover's watchful eye.

Back at the hotel, he found Abe. He was alone, leaning against the wall, watching the street.

"Sounds like you've been busy," he said after hearing Shad's account of the search and his encounter with Glover.

"Busy, maybe, but nothing to show for it."

"Well, the way I heard it, them fellows hung around here from time to time. For them to ride into town and disappear like that, somebody local has got to be helping them out."

"For a cut of the gold, no doubt."

"Looks like. Now, who might be willing to do something like that?"

This started Shad to thinking about their earlier visit to Cimarron. They'd stopped at the saloon where Schultz was the barkeep. Later, it was Schultz's name that the outlaw, Scott, had mentioned before the shootout. It was also Schultz who had a pretty wife with expensive taste. She was the kind of woman who required a lot of money to keep her in style.

He told Abe what he was thinking.

"Sounds to me like you might be barking up the right tree, son. I expect we ought to keep an eye on Mr. Schultz."

Shad remembered something else. "Lark mentioned that his wife has a fancy carriage. Bet she has a place to park it out of the elements, too."

"If you're right, they're apt to be guarding that place with a lot of firepower."

"Then come dark, I might wander over that way and have a look."

"Not by yourself, you won't. I've come too far to be left out now. I'm betting Lurvey's going to want to deal himself in on this, too."

"Fine. The more the better. But it'd be a good idea for us to leave the hotel one by one. I don't want anybody noticing what we're up to, like that scrawny desk clerk."

"This is an expensive place," said Abe. "I hope we

don't have to hole up here much longer. Soft living is spoiling me."

"Not much danger of you getting spoiled," said Shad, giving him a sideways glance. "But I know a gal who might like to try."

"Larkspur's got a mind of her own, but I guess I'll have to take care not to get myself shot tonight."

The thought of getting shot at again was sobering.

Chapter Ten

Shad lay sprawled on his bed in the hotel room, waiting for darkness. Minutes were slowly turning into hours when a knock sounded at the door.

"Hold on a minute!" he called.

He swung his feet to the floor, pulled on his boots, and went to see who was there. To his surprise, he found Inez Schultz filling the doorway. Her earrings sparkled, her cheeks were flushed, and she reeked of perfume. An expression of impatience crossed her face. Apparently she hadn't liked waiting. Before speaking, he stuck his head out and looked down the hall. It appeared she'd come alone.

"I'd like a few minutes of your time, Mr. Wakefield," she said, her voice sultry. "Aren't you going to invite me into your room?" She knew his name.

This evening she was wearing a different dress than the one he'd seen her in earlier. It was pale blue, a color that flattered her eyes, with a cut that flattered her figure. She carried a matching reticule, the kind of handbag

131

that was handy for concealing things like derringers. He wondered what she was doing here, what she wanted with him. He'd seen her type before and he was wary.

"What can I do for you, Mrs. Schultz?" he asked. "I must say, I'm surprised that a lady such as yourself would visit my hotel room unescorted."

She smiled coquettishly, showing deep dimples.

"There's no need for you to be prudish, Mr. Wakefield. It's just that there's been a little misunderstanding that I'd like to discuss with you."

In spite of her smile, her eyes were as cold as the Picketwire in winter. This woman was up to no good. He could feel it in his bones. While she meant to be disarming, she was having the opposite effect. She reminded him of a poisonous snake that was getting ready to strike death to its victim.

"I'm afraid I don't know what misunderstanding you're talking about, Mrs. Schultz."

"It's my husband. I'm afraid that you've upset him very much. May I come in so that we can talk in private?"

Shad didn't like this one bit. No respectable married woman would do such a thing. She was intent on causing trouble.

"One moment," he said. He brushed past her into the hall, went over and rapped sharply on the door of Lark's room.

"Shad, what's wrong?" Lark asked when she saw the look on his face.

"Mrs. Schultz is here and she wants to come into my room for a private talk. Would you kindly join us?"

She glanced down the hall at the barkeep's wife. Inez Schultz's sultry expression had turned to one of undisguised fury.

"Of course," said Lark pleasantly. "I'd be delighted to join you."

The Schultz woman clutched her reticule and threw them both a look of pure hatred.

"Never mind," she said. "When I told you I wanted to talk to you privately, Mr. Wakefield, I meant privately."

In a swish of skirt and petticoats, she brushed passed them and stormed down the stairs.

"Now, what was all that about?" asked Lark.

He shrugged. "I don't know, but I wanted no part of it."

"That woman is mixed up in this business the same as her husband," said Lark. "I wouldn't be surprised if she'd planned to shoot you. Afterward, she'd probably claim that you lured her into your room and attacked her. She'd tell everyone she had to kill you in self-defense, shoot you to defend her honor. It'd be a quick, sure means of getting you out of the way for good."

It made sense to Shad. "It's likely," he agreed. "Whatever she had in mind, I wasn't buying. Thanks for your help."

"Shad," she said, gently touching his arm, "be careful. For them to pull a nasty stunt like this, it means you've got them plenty worried."

"I expect you're right. I'll keep alert."

He returned to his room where the scent of perfume lingered in the doorway. No longer could he stand the bed or a chair, for he was restless. His nerves were taut and geared up for trouble. What would they try next? He went to the window and looked out onto the street.

Below, the saloons were beginning to fill up for the evening. A late-season wagon train had stopped that afternoon, near the town. It was taking a brief rest before continuing on its way to Independence. *Could this be how Todd intended to get the gold out*? He considered the possibility, but it didn't seem likely. The wagon master wouldn't be taking on more wagons along the trail. That was, if the outlaws had them, which they obviously didn't. But what if a couple of those wagons in the train were empty, or mostly empty, waiting for their cargo of gold? Could Todd have planned something so intricate? He doubted it. First of all, the cargos would have been checked. A wagon without any cargo, or very little, would have aroused suspicion. Second, Todd wasn't sure until the last minute when the gold was to be shipped. Shad felt confident he could rule out the wagon train.

There was another problem. It was almost time for them to be underway, and it didn't look like Lurvey was going to show up. They could have used him. Toby was a kid with an injured wing and Lark was a woman. It was going to be left up to him and Abe.

As soon as twilight had deepened into night, Shad strapped on his pistol and picked up the rifle. Then he went across the hall and knocked lightly on Abe's door.

"It's time," he said when Abe opened it.

"Figured it was. I've been waiting."

Abe stepped into the hall and closed the door behind him.

"Lurvey's not here," said Shad. "It'll be the two of us."

"I hope he didn't run into trouble. I kind of liked him."

If Lurvey had gotten himself into trouble, he was going to have to get himself out of it. Shad figured he was as savvy as anybody.

They walked past the closed door of Lark's room.

"I guess you told Toby that he's not going to be in on this," said Shad when they got to the head of the stairs.

"Not exactly. But I told him if anything happened to us to hightail it back to the ranch. Seein' his pa is his main concern. It's the reason we came down here in the first place."

In the lobby, a clock chimed the half hour. Shad paused. "You know, if I were Todd and knew folks like us were on my trail, I'd have somebody out there, watching the front door."

"You mean someone with that 'malicious intent' you was talking about?"

"Precisely."

At that hour, the downstairs was empty except for the haughty desk clerk. But tonight he was perched behind the admissions desk making a big pretense of minding his own business.

"Wait here," Shad told his partner in a low voice. "I'm going out the back way. Keep an eye on that fellow."

There was a chance they'd have the back door watched, too, but it wasn't so likely. He entered an unlit storage room and struck a match. A door at the other end led outside. He snuffed the match and opened the door wide enough to slip out. Then he moved quickly away. The alley was black as pitch. He was feeling his way along the rough wall of the building when suddenly he tripped and fell. Someone had dumped a pile of adobe bricks out back. Rubbing his sore knee, he swore softly. Then he listened for a moment, his hand near the grips of his pistol. If anyone was in the alley and heard him fall, they were making no sound. He got to his feet and slipped around the side of the building, stopping just short of the front corner of the hotel. Here, he had a clear view of the street and nearby businesses. At first he saw nothing amiss. Then he spotted it—a glint of moonlight on steel. A sniper. He was hidden across the street in the space between buildings. If he and Abe had walked out the front door of the hotel, they'd have been shot down.

He needed to draw the gunman out. Make him show his hand. Quietly, he retraced his steps to the brick pile and grabbed one. Back at his hiding place, he checked to see that the man was still there. All that was visible was a shadowy silhouette. It was enough. He drew back and hurled the adobe missile. There was a *thunk* and a yelp before the gun discharged wildly. Saloon doors flew open as patrons poured onto the boardwalk to see what had happened. Marshal Glover appeared in front of the jail. Discovered, the sniper ran. Shad sprinted after him. Onlookers blocked the way. Shad pushed through and tackled him, throwing him to the ground. He was struggling to get loose when Glover arrived.

"Give it up," the marshal ordered. "I've got you covered."

Shad backed off while Glover disarmed the gunman and dragged him into the light that spilled from a saloon. It was Bledsoe.

"Are you drunk?" Glover asked. "Shooting off your pistol like that, you could've killed somebody."

"He's not drunk," said Shad. "This is one of the fellows who robbed the gold shipment. He was waiting over there to bushwhack me and my partner when we left the hotel. His name is Bledsoe."

"I see. Well, we have a nice room for him down at the jail. I expect there's some big shot mining fellows who'd like to have a talk with him."

"I'm not a big shot mining fellow," said Shad, "but I'd like for him to answer some questions. If you don't mind, I'll tag along."

"Sure. Just don't get in the way."

Glover was shoving a path through the large gathering of onlookers, keeping Bledsoe in front of him. Shad was left to follow in their wake. Suddenly, from out of the crowd, there was a popping sound. It was immediately followed by another. There was a scream. Panic and pandemonium spread like wildfire. Bledsoe slumped against Glover, who caught him and eased him down. Blood stained the front of the outlaw's shirt and gun smoke tainted the air.

"Who shot him?" the marshal demanded. "Did anybody see anything?"

He got no answer from the scattered crowd, but Shad had seen plenty. While they were moving toward the jail, he'd caught a glimpse of a woman in the moonlight. Her shawl had fallen back and her blond hair gleamed like a moonflower. Inez Schultz had moved in close with the onlookers. There she'd managed to shoot Bledsoe. From the sound of it, she must have used a two-shot derringer. He recalled the way the woman had looked when she came to his room. He'd noticed that her reticule was on the heavy side from the way she'd carried it. Of course, it could have been full of silver dollars, but he'd have bet on a lady's pistol over dollars. Inez Schultz was, without question, a dangerous woman.

The marshal enlisted help to carry the wounded man to the jail. Shad followed along behind and was soon joined by his partner.

"Looks like Mrs. Schultz was scared he'd talk," said Abe.

"I guess you spotted her, too."

"Yeah. Lark told me what she tried to do to you. Appears to me that our gold thieves are worried."

"We've got a problem," said Shad. "She's guilty as sin but still, we can't go around accusing a respectable woman of attempted murder. That might not set too well with the people here in Cimarron."

"I expect you're right. Best we keep it to ourselves for awhile."

Shad noticed that the Schultz woman had a knack for disappearing when she wanted to. There was nary a sign of her.

They put the wounded man on a cot in one of the cells and sent for the doctor. Bledsoe was still conscious, but blood was flowing from a chest wound. Shad went over and knelt down beside him.

"Bledsoe, listen to me. Once you got arrested, they were afraid you'd talk. The Schultz woman shot you."

"I know," he said after a pained breath. "She shouldn't've done it. I wouldn't have talked. Get a doc. Please. I hurt something awful."

Tomlin rushed in with his bag.

"He's over there," said the marshal.

Shad moved back out of the way and watched as the doctor tore open Bledsoe's bloody shirt.

"A derringer at close range does a lot of damage," said Shad.

"You were there?"

"Right behind him, along with the marshal. Bledsoe took both bullets."

Tomlin shook his head. "No use probing for them. It'd be a waste of time. There's nothing left to do but make him comfortable."

Shad stared down at the wounded outlaw. Whether he'd heard or not, he couldn't tell. The man had the smell of death about him.

"Look, before the end, I need to talk to him."

"Then you'd better do it fast," said Tomlin.

He knelt close to the outlaw's ear, aware that this was the man who'd given him the beating at Last Chance.

"Bledsoe, listen to me. Do you really think Todd was going to give you part of that gold when he could get rid of you and keep your share for himself? How many ways is it going to be divided? Todd? Mohler? Their contact here in Cimarron? The woman who shot you? Do you think they'll cut in Thurman? Or Strong, for that matter, if he's still alive? The fewer ways that gold is divided, the more there is for the ones who remain. Tell me where they're headed."

Bledsoe's breathing was ragged. He struggled to form a word.

"Ascension," he gasped. Then his eyes glazed over and his raspy breathing stopped.

"He's all done in," said Doc Tomlin as he pulled the blanket over the dead outlaw's face. "Did you report the woman who did the shooting?"

"No," said Shad. "I can't go accusing her. She has standing in the community."

"Reckon I can guess who you're talking about," said Glover, "even though I didn't see her. From what I hear, there's a lot of people in this town who wouldn't be at all surprised if you was to say her name."

So the marshal was admitting that he and a lot of others knew, or at least suspected, Inez Schultz for what she was—an avaricious, cold-blooded killer.

"There's a big carriage house on the Schultz property, out past the edge of town," said Glover, propping his foot on the rung of a stool. "The place is screened on this side by a row of Russian olive trees. Nobody would be able to see what was going on there unless they rode right past it. Maybe not even then, if whatever was going on was inside the place. It might be interesting to ride out there and take a look at what's in that carriage house. Bet it's not that fancy phaeton of hers."

Shad had a feeling the marshal was right.

"Why don't you go on out there and have a look, Glover?" said Doc Tomlin. "After all, you're the law."

"Because, strictly speaking, it's outside of town and, therefore, outside of my jurisdiction. Not to mention I'd likely get shot at, and I'm not taking any lead for a bunch of rich mine owners. They don't pay my salary. If you're thinking of the sheriff, he's out on a manhunt. Let Rossman Blair and his two partners do their own fighting, or else hire it done."

So that's the way it was, not that Shad could much blame him. It was still up to him and Abe.

"Looks like you'd want to arrest that Schultz woman for murder," said Abe. "It seems to me that the main street of Cimarron is, sure enough, in your jurisdiction."

Glover glanced down at Bledsoe's body. "Afraid I can't go making arrests on a stranger's say so, and none of the others saw her shoot him, else they'd have been in here squawking their heads off."

What it added up to was Marshal Glover was a cautious man. Maybe something of a politician. He knew Inez Schultz for what she was. He admitted that others suspected, as well. Still, he wouldn't risk arresting her for murder. It might be that he was afraid of taking a bullet like Bledsoe had done.

The woman had been quick and discreet, Shad would give her that. While everyone's attention was focused on the marshal and his prisoner, she'd been able to blend into the crowd and kill without being noticed. Afterward, it was an easy matter for her to slip away as if she'd never been there.

Shad made ready to leave the jail. "Well, Marshal, I don't have to worry about jurisdiction since I don't have any. But I do owe Todd for ordering a beating and for locking me in a shed until he could get a chance to kill me. The rest of 'em I owe for what they did to a couple of friends of mine. I don't intend to waste any more time."

"Then I wish you good hunting," said Glover. "Watch your back."

When Shad left the jail, Abe was right behind him. They retrieved their horses and rode out south to the Schultz place. The big, whitewashed house looked ghostly in the moonlight. Not so much as a single candle relieved the darkness inside.

"It don't look like anybody's at home," said Abe. "If that woman knows you saw her, she probably went to warn her husband. She might be hiding out with him so that nobody can ask her any questions."

Shad agreed that this was likely.

"I've got a feeling this place is empty," he said. "I

have a hunch the outlaws were here and that they've pulled out."

They tied the horses and went to have a look around back. There they found the carriage house.

"Good grief," said Abe. "That woman could have sheltered three or four rigs in there."

"I guess Mrs. Schultz is looking forward to a prosperous future."

When Shad lifted the heavy wooden bar from the door and pulled it open, the stench from inside nearly knocked him backward.

"Guess we've found where they hid the mules."

"Looks like," said Abe, "but them poor critters that they brought from the mountains would've been all done in. They probably had some others waiting here."

Then the question was, how did they dispose of the first team?

Shad scratched a match on the bottom of his boot and had a look. The floor was clean of animal waste, but the odor remained. Just as the flame was about to reach his fingers, he spotted a lantern on a shelf near the door. He blew out the match and struck another. With the second, he lit the lantern. Now he could see all of the interior. The purple phaeton was parked there in all its glory. Four wagon wheels leaned against the west wall. Nearby was a saw and some other tools. He dropped to one knee for a closer look and found tiny slivers of wood that had escaped the broom.

"Guess this is where that gold wagon ended its days," said Abe.

"It appears they took the thing apart. We'd best have a look outside."

Shad led the way, carrying the lantern. Its light was hidden from town by the thick screen of low-growing trees. It didn't take them long to find where an area of dirt had recently been disturbed.

"There was a shovel inside that carriage house," said Abe. "I'll be right back."

When he reappeared, he had not one shovel, but two. They made short work of uncovering the wagon pieces as well as the remains of a mule. Only one mule. The others must have been in good enough shape to go on.

"Do you reckon that Bledsoe was telling the truth and they're really headed for that Ascension town down in Mexico?" asked Abe.

Shad had given the dying man's last word some thought.

"No," he said. "They may have told Bledsoe that's where they were going, but think about it. To go to Ascension, they'd have to swing to the west and cross the *Jornada del Muerto*. That's eighty miles without a sign of water. On top of that, it would put them in Mescalero country. There's not many of the outlaws left and there's a whole lot of Apaches."

"So you don't buy it."

"Nope. But I do think they're headed south. They wouldn't go by the main trail, though. Too risky."

"Why not north?"

"They'd have to go through the pass. Again, they'd be too easy to spot."

"I expect you're right, son. Why don't we throw a few shovelfuls of dirt over that carcass and go after 'em."

In answer, Shad hefted the shovel and went to work covering up what they'd just uncovered.

They finished quickly and rode back to the hotel to collect their things. Lark's door was shut and Abe said he didn't want to disturb her. They decided it was best not to tell Toby, either. At the livery stable, Abe put the blaze on a lead line, along with the *gruello* that had belonged to Scott. The hostler, a round-faced, pleasant-looking man, was still there in spite of the lateness of the hour.

"Heard the goings-on out on the street awhile ago. Know anything about it?"

Shad answered for them. "A prisoner got shot at close range before the marshal could get him to the jail. The killer got away."

The hostler shook his head. "You can't never tell what's going to happen around here any more."

As they were about to leave, Abe paused.

"Look," he said. "if I write out a note, would you take it to a lady at the hotel in the morning? Be glad to pay you."

"I'd be happy to do it. No charge. Write 'er up."

Abe fished in his pocket for a stub of a pencil and a scrap of paper.

"Are you sure you don't want to go back and tell Lark in person?" said Shad. "She and Toby aren't going to like it that we rode off this way."

"I don't want any arguments. And I sure don't want 'em tagging along. Anything could happen. This is the best way. Trust me."

He finished scribbling the note and handed it into the keeping of the hostler.

"I'm obliged to you," he said. "She'd worry if she didn't get this."

"She'll get it," he promised.

On their way out of town, Shad noticed that Schultz's saloon was brightly lit and noisy as usual.

"Do you reckon that woman's somewhere inside that place?" said Abe.

"Probably. They've got a lot to lose here in Cimarron. That fancy house. A profitable saloon. It could be they'll stay and try to brazen it out."

"Woman's got plenty of gall, that's for sure."

On that, Shad could agree. They soon left Cimarron behind, and by the light of the moon they rode southward on a lonely trail toward the town of Rayado.

Chapter Eleven

It was fully daylight when they approached the shallow wash. Even before Shad could see it, he could smell the smoldering remains of the fire that had burned within. It hadn't been the small campfire of somebody passing through, either. There was the distinct odor of burnt flesh. When they neared the edge, the horses shied. They wanted no part of this place. Shad prodded the dun forward until he could see what lay below the rim.

Abe drew up beside him. "Well, Shadrach, I guess we know what happened to them wore-out mules."

The wash contained the animals' charred remains.

At first light, they'd spotted the tracks of five horses and eleven mules. The trail led straight to this wash, where the outlaws had rid themselves of the team that had hauled the gold from Last Chance. It looked like they'd shot them and delivered them to the flames. The gold was being packed out on the backs of the fresh replacements, the ones that had been held in waiting at the Schultz place.

They crossed the wash, skirting the remains of the fire. On the other side, the mule tracks were sunk deep, testifying to the weight of their burden.

"They're heavy laden," said Abe, "but I still don't think they're carrying it all."

Shad was thinking the same thing. "You might be right. Todd may have stashed some of it back in Cimarron, planning to sneak in and retrieve it later."

"Another thing," said Abe. "There's five of 'em. That means Todd and Mohler for sure. That red-headed Thurman. Strong, who's wounded. But who is the fifth?"

"Schultz, I guess. Who else could it be? We know they left the woman and Bledsoe in town."

Abe looked unconvinced. "Odd. I wouldn't have expected Schultz to leave town at all. Not with his business to take care of."

"Maybe it wasn't his own idea to leave. A man will do a lot of things with a gun in his back. Could be that Inez Schultz figured she'd like it better as a widow."

Abe shook his head. "Some women have dark souls. I figure hers is about as black as they come."

He wasn't getting an argument on that.

The outlaws' trail didn't go into Rayado, but circled around it instead. A couple of miles to the south, it intercepted the wide Santa Fe Trade Route. This was well used, with lots of tracks, ruts, and animal droppings. Here, amidst the jumble, the outlaws merged their tracks with the others. There was no sign of them up ahead, either, despite the fact that the land was open and it was possible to see for a great distance.

"What now?" asked his partner.

"We ride along and watch for signs where they turned off the trade route, for that's what they had to do."

Abe thought about it. "You know, if Bledsoe was telling the truth and their destination really is that town down in Mexico, they might head south and swing around through the Glorietta Pass before turning south again."

"They might. But I still think Ascension was a lot of hogwash. Nothing but a tale told to Bledsoe to throw us off in case he talked. If you want my opinion, Todd's soft. He's not man enough to tackle the *Jornada*, which means at least four days' journey without water. That's not counting all the hostile Apaches he's apt to encounter on the way. Besides, if he had to leave part of the shipment behind, he's not going to want to get that far away from it."

"Putting it that way, it makes a lot of sense," Abe admitted.

The *Sangre de Cristos* lay off in the distance to Shad's right, and he knew that Ocate Creek was somewhere up ahead. Beyond the creek was the Turkey Mountains. They rode in silence for most of an hour before he reined up.

"There," he said pointing to where the tracks of half a dozen mules and five horses turned off. "They're headed west, back toward the *Sangres*."

"By gum, you was right all along, Shadrach. They're no more going to Mexico than they're flying to thunder."

"They're not trying to cover their trail anymore, either. Guess they're not worried. We'd better get moving."

Going without sleep for part of a day, a night, and

another day was taking a toll. Shad was nodding in the saddle when they made camp in the Turkey Mountains. September was almost gone, and before long the cottonwoods would be yellowing up in the river bottoms. They spread their blankets on the lee side, under a bluff, and kept the small campfire fed. At daybreak, they prepared to leave.

"Since them fellows ain't going on down to Mexico," said Abe, "could it be they're headed for Mora?"

Shad had heard of the old town. Mora was a tight-knit community, mostly made up of descendants of the early settlers who'd come up the *Camino Real* from Mexico many years before.

"I doubt if that's their destination," he said. "They won't want to attract any notice, and if Todd and a bunch of *gringos* were to go riding into Mora with those heavy laden pack mules, they'd stand out like a bloody nose. Some of the good citizens might be curious enough to use force in finding out what's in those packs. Todd has to know this. No, it's more likely he's got a hideout in the mountains. Someplace where they can lay low until it's safe to divide the stuff and go their separate ways. That is, if Todd intends to divide it."

"Well, it's sure not going to be hard to find 'em. Not with the kind of trail they're leaving behind now. It's like they don't expect to be followed any more."

Shad believed he knew the answer to that. "They're aware of Marshal Glover's reluctance to leave his jurisdiction. They must also have heard that the sheriff is off hunting a killer."

"I don't reckon that Todd and Mohler have much respect for our staying power either," said Abe.

"They were counting on Bledsoe to put an end to us. They've got no way of knowing that he failed."

That they weren't expected provided a small edge. A badly needed one. Shad and his partner pushed on. The following day found them high in the *Sangre de Cristos*. The tall peak of *Cerro Vista* lay to the north. A stiff breeze forced its way through the pines and rattled the aspen leaves. Once, Shad caught a glimpse of a magnificent buck that bounded away when he caught the scent of horses and men. This was wild country. Sheer beauty. But his instincts warned of danger. He had a feeling they were getting close to their quarry, and the outlaws outnumbered them more than two to one.

Single-file, they followed a trail that looked ancient. Probably it had been made by animals or by a people long gone. The wind gusted and Shad caught the scent of wood smoke. He reined up and glanced back at his partner. Abe had smelled it, too.

"It's coming from over that way," he said, pointing to his right.

They followed their noses until they were able to spot the hideout. Making sure they were screened by trees, they stopped and looked the place over. A fair-sized cabin sat in a small clearing. It was a ramshackle affair, but usable. A plume of smoke rose from its chimney. Nearby, a corral was filled with mules. The outlaws' horses were hitched in front of the cabin.

"Well, son, I'd say we've found ourselves a nest of rattlers," said Abe. "The question is, what do we do about it?"

"For now, we wait. When we move in, we'd best do it after nightfall."

"I go along with you there, Shadrach. We wouldn't stand much of a chance if we start something now."

Just then the cabin door opened and one of the outlaws appeared. He headed for the woodpile.

"It's Schultz," said Abe. "Well, that answers my question about the last man. Your hunch about the barkeep was right."

While they watched, Schultz picked up an axe and started chopping wood. It was a hard, menial task and it made clear exactly where the man stood in the outlaws' pecking order.

Mohler stepped outside and yelled at the paunchy barkeep loud enough for Shad to hear.

"Hurry up! We need that wood right now!"

Shad waited for his reaction, but the smaller man only swung the axe faster.

Satisfied, Mohler went back inside.

"Nice fellow," said Abe under his breath. They both knew there was nothing nice or decent about the outlaw boss.

Without a backward glance, they withdrew to a safer distance to await nightfall.

"It would've been a big help if Lurvey had gotten back in time to come with us," said Abe as he lay on the grass under the shade of a pine. "We sure could use another man. Lurvey was lookin' in the wrong place, trying to find something that wasn't there."

That happens sometimes, Shad thought. But the mine owners' agent didn't appear to have the best instincts.

"We can't worry about Lurvey now," he said. "There's just the two of us, and we'll do what we have to."

"That's the way it usually is. Can't count on strangers."

Whenever Shad was waiting for something to happen, time always crept along at a snail's pace. It did so now. But at last, the sun dipped behind the mountains and the stars came out. He got to his feet.

"I'd say it's time to go," he said. "We'll separate and come at 'em from both sides at an angle. That way we'll be out of each other's line of fire."

"Sounds like the best way to me."

They split up near the edge of the clearing. Abe went to one side, taking the spare horses with him, while Shad circled around to the other. When he heard the squeak of the cabin door swinging open, he drew up and watched. One of the outlaws came out and looked around. He was back-lit by a lantern, and even from a distance, Shad could tell it was Thurman. He was carrying a rifle.

"Red, you're getting jumpier than an old woman," came Mohler's voice from inside the hideout.

"You can say what you want to. But I ain't aiming to get caught with my britches down. I've got a bad feeling and I'm going to have a look around."

Shad remained motionless. He was thankful that Squire was well trained. Thurman moved out to the edge of the clearing and made around of its circumference. At one point, the outlaw turned and looked straight in Shad's direction. He seemed to sense something. But Shad was well-concealed by trees and darkness. After a moment, the outlaw turned and went back inside. Shad expelled the breath he hadn't realized he'd been holding.

Unimpressive though it was, the cabin acted as a fortress, the clearing as a moat. In order to capture the gold robbers, he'd have to lure them outside. He released the thong on the butt of his revolver and placed the rifle across his knees. Then he rode in closer. When he was established, he imitated the hooting sound of a night owl. The light that spilled from underneath the door went out. Inside, they'd heard the bird-call and were suspicious. The next move was theirs. A minute passed, then two. Finally, the door of the cabin squeaked open. Someone looked out, but he was cautious and not exposing himself to gunfire.

"You in there!" Shad called. "You're surrounded!"

The door slammed shut.

"Better give it up, Todd!" he yelled.

There was no sound. It was likely that Todd and Mohler were trying to decide what to do. They'd been taken by surprise. No doubt of that. After giving them a couple of minutes, he shouted again.

"All of you, come out with your hands in the air! There's plenty of moonlight for me to see by, so don't try anything foolish!"

A curse was followed by a gunshot. Shad, expecting their reaction, had moved to another spot the instant he'd spoken. The shot caused no harm, but it opened the ball. The outlaws were all firing from inside the cabin. A couple were stationed at the window, where the shutters were pulled open. The others were firing from the doorway. All together, they were lying down a volley, hoping for a lucky hit. From the woods on the other side, Abe had begun to wage his own battle. The outlaws' attention was divided.

Shad took aim at the window and squeezed off a shot. There was a sudden outcry. His bullet had found a target.

"I've got you now!" shouted Thurman.

Shad glanced over to his left and saw the shadowy form of the outlaw. He was scarcely more than a dozen yards away. He'd gotten out the back and had made his way around through the forest. Now that he had Shad in his sights, Red Beard was taking his time in order to savor the moment. With the outlaw's gun on him, he had no chance to draw the .44, or to bring the rifle to bear. This might well be the last moment of his life. His mind raced. Nearby was a growth of underbrush. It wasn't much of a chance, but it was his only one. He kicked his feet loose from the stirrups and dove for cover, rolling as soon as he hit the ground. A bullet dug in, close to his hand, sending up dirt and pine needles.

"You can't get away from me, Wakefield!" Thurman called. "You're a fool to even try."

Shad brought up the rifle and tried to get off a shot. It wouldn't fire. His lunge for cover had somehow damaged it.

The outlaw fired again and again, searching for his unseen target. Shad scrambled deeper into the brush. His hand gripped the butt of his pistol, the one that had belonged to Thurman. He was lifting it to shoot, when something slammed into his side. It felt like a stab of fire. Thurman had found his mark.

Shad squeezed off a shot of his own but Thurman had moved aside.

"I've got him!" he yelled to his partners in the cabin.

Not yet, you don't.

Crab-like, he crawled farther back in the brush, trying not to make any sound that would give him away. His shirt was moist with blood. How badly he'd been hit, he couldn't tell.

All the shooting from the cabin had stopped. Even Abe's gun was silent.

"Tell him we've got the old man!" came Todd's voice. "If he doesn't come in we'll kill him."

"Don't you do it, Shadrach!" Abe yelled. This was followed by a silence that was ominous.

One thing he knew. Once he surrendered, they were both dead. Their only chance was for him to get away.

"Come on out here where I can see you, Wakefield," said Thurman. "If you don't, I'll start shooting again."

Shad retreated deeper into cover. His situation was bad. He knew that. Wounded and on foot, there was little chance for survival. As soon as he left the saddle, Squire had run off. Suddenly, there was the sound of running footfalls. Someone had come from the cabin.

"Where is he?" asked Mohler, puffing loudly from the exertion.

"He's in that underbrush somewhere."

Shad lay perfectly still. To attract attention now would be fatal. His breathing became shallow, and he was thankful that they didn't have a dog to sniff him out.

"Maybe you plugged him," said Mohler. "Maybe he's lying dead in there someplace."

"Could be, but I ain't tramping through that stuff tonight. If we're wrong, I could get a piece of lead in my belly. If you want to try it, though, you're more'n welcome."

There was a pause, as if, Mohler was considering it. Then he uttered a sound that was almost a growl.

"All right," said Thurman. "Daylight, then."

They turned and went back to the cabin.

The shock of having been shot was wearing off now.

Shad's side was hurting like it was on fire, and he felt like throwing up. He explored with his hand. It came away wet. Stripping off his bandana, he folded it and pressed it over the wound to stanch the blood flow. Then he drew his shirt tight across to hold it in place. He couldn't tell for sure, but with luck, the bullet had passed through without damaging any vital organs. Nonetheless, he could bleed to death if he wasn't careful. In spite of that fact, he had to get moving. Time was limited. He had only until daybreak to find Squire and figure out how to rescue Abe.

Chapter Twelve

As soon as the outlaws had gone, Shad struggled to his feet. He felt dizzy and shook his head to clear it. Then he checked his side again. The bandana bandage was working. The bleeding had almost stopped.

He tried hard to focus his mind and assess his situation. The rifle was no use to him. All he had was that fancy Smith and Wesson .44 that he'd taken from Thurman the night he'd happened on the outlaws' camp. Worse, he didn't have much ammunition left.

From the cabin came the sound of the shutters and the door being slammed shut. The gang was holing up for the night. Inside that cabin, Abe was their prisoner. No doubt he was hurt. Shad risked a low whistle for Squire. Nothing. The dun was gone. He had until daylight before the outlaws swept across the area, hunting him down like a wild animal. In his condition, it wouldn't be hard for them to do. Ignoring the pain as best he could, he put one foot in front of the other and forced himself to walk away. He managed to make several yards before he had to stop and steady himself against a tree. Ripping a piece of flannel from his shirt, he added it to the packing in his wound. No sense in leaving a blood trail for them to follow.

Step by step he made progress, but it was painfully slow. He wished for the moccasins that were packed in his saddle bag. They'd disturb the ground far less than the boots he was wearing. He might just as well wish for the moon.

It was vital to put distance between himself and the outlaws' hideout. Each stop for rest was a luxury he couldn't afford. The pines rose up around him like giants in the night, their needles playing a wind-song that might well become a dirge. Shad wasn't thinking straight and was aware that he was fading in and out of consciousness. Time had become a murky concept. So had distance. Once when he sat down to rest, he realized that he had no idea how far he'd come or how long it had taken. His only measurement was the shift of his weight from one foot to the other, the steps he'd failed to count. He hauled himself up and staggered on. Then there was blessed blackness as the measuring stopped.

As he drifted toward wakefulness, Shad became aware of the cold. It had penetrated every part of his body and was causing him to shiver uncontrollably. It took him a few minutes to remember where he was and what had brought him to this sorry state of affairs. With effort, he got to his knees. It was then he heard a nicker from somewhere in the dark.

"Squire?"

On hearing his voice, the horse trotted over and nudged him.

"Good boy, you found me," he said. He stood on shaky legs and grabbed hold of the horse's mane to steady himself. Then, putting his foot in the stirrup, he swung into the saddle.

His situation was a little brighter now. He had the things he needed. There was water, food, a coat, ammunition, and even a little whiskey to clean his wound. He shrugged into the coat and took a drink from his canteen.

There was no telling how long he'd lain unconscious on the ground. The outlaws would be looking for him as soon as it was light enough to see. It was important to cover his tracks from now on, at least as best he could. Not that it would be an easy task in the dark. As he proceeded, he drew on every trick he knew. The next few hours would decide his fate and that of his long-time friend.

He rode through the night, using the stars to guide him and keep him from going in circles. When there was enough pre-dawn light to see by, he reined up and pulled the whiskey bottle from a saddlebag. Gingerly, he opened his shirt and removed the blood-soaked packing. Then, teeth clenched, he drenched the wound with whiskey. The pain was so bad that it was all he could do to keep from crying out. When it receded to dull a throb, he found a clean neck-scarf and used it to replace the other. Then he wrapped it with a bandage that he carried in his supplies.

He worried about Abe. Most likely the outlaws would keep him alive on the off chance they'd need him for bait. But his voice had been cut off abruptly. He'd probably been hit.

When Shad was through doctoring his wound, he

mounted up. At least his head was clear now, and he didn't have to worry about losing consciousness and falling out of the saddle. The murky gray receded, giving way to the fiery orange disc that shed light and warmth. Soon he was able to pull off the pale-colored duster, roll it, and stuff it away. His dull green shirt, mutilated though it was, would be hard to spot in a forest of the same color. The dun blended into the background, as well.

He'd done his best to cover his trail, but he wasn't sure it'd be enough. Time would soon tell. He swung back to the south, intending to come up on the opposite side of the cabin. He'd learned that doing the unexpected always gave a man the edge.

A bright blue mountain jay flew low, directly across his path. Its suddenness startled the horse.

"Steady, boy," Shad soothed. "Guess that fellow forgot his manners."

From time to time, he stopped to listen. The densely-needled tree branches made it impossible to watch his back trail. He was forced to rely on his ears. As he drew closer to the cabin, he wondered which of the outlaws had gone looking for him, and which had stayed behind to guard their prisoner.

At last, he reached a place where he could see the cabin through the trees. Abe's horses were there, along with the *gruello* he'd been using as a spare. Besides these, there were three others. That meant two of the outlaws had gone after him. He'd hoped to find that they'd all gone, leaving Abe tied up and alone. But he hadn't really expected it. There wasn't going to be an easy out.

He moved in closer. Looking down, he spotted a

single hoof print in a patch of dirt. Nearby, there were brush strokes as if someone had tried to wipe out his tracks with a tree branch. Shad froze, all of his senses alert. Whoever had wiped those tracks was dug in somewhere on the slope above, waiting for him. If he'd missed seeing that single track, he would have ridden straight into an outlaw's gunsights.

Squire had caught the scent of the other horses, and being a sociable creature, he was eager to go down to them. Shad reined him back.

"You can't go yet, boy," he said, keeping his voice low. "We've got some other work to do first."

Lark was deeply troubled as she made her way downstairs to the hotel lobby. First of all, Abe hadn't come back from the Schultz place. Neither had Shad. When she went to check on them, she found their rooms were empty.

From her own room at the back of the building, she hadn't been able to see what was happening on the street the night before. But she could hear, and she could have sworn she heard a gunshot. Before coming downstairs, she'd stopped and knocked on Toby's door. When he finally made an appearance, he was tousled and half asleep. It turned out that he didn't know any more about what had happened than she did.

When she got to the lobby, the desk clerk got up and approached her. He was carrying a scrap of paper.

"Miss Russell, the hostler left this for you a little while ago."

"Thank you," she said, accepting it from his hand. She hastily read Abe's scrawled note and was scarcely finished when Toby came bounding down the stairs.

"What do you think happened?" he asked, now fully awake.

She was mad and finding it hard to control her temper.

"According to this piece of scribbling, the two of them took off on their own last night without telling us. They're on the trail of the outlaws."

"Are you sure?" Toby asked.

She nodded.

Now it was his turn to be angry. "We can't let them get away with that. We're in on this, too. We've got to go after 'em."

She squared her shoulders and lifted a determined chin. "That's my thought, exactly, Toby. We'll have some breakfast and then get started. But first I want to have a few words with the desk clerk."

She approached him and asked if he knew anything about the gunshot she'd heard the night before.

He looked at her over his spectacles and cleared his throat.

"Why, yes," he said. "It seems that a fellow was waiting across the street to shoot somebody as they came out of the hotel last night. He missed. The marshal arrested him, and when he was taking the shooter to jail, somebody in the crowd killed him at close range with two shots from a derringer."

"I'm afraid I didn't hear those last two shots, but then I was on the backside of the hotel and they're not all that loud. Can you tell me the dead man's name?"

"I believe they said it was Bledsoe. He was supposed to have worked up at one of the mining camps. A security officer, I think."

Todd's *segundo*. The one who'd given Shad a beating. "Were they able to catch the person who shot him?"

The desk clerk shook his head.

"No. Like I said, a crowd had gathered. After the first shot was fired, everyone came running to see what was going on. Nobody was expecting a prisoner to be shot down while he was literally in the marshal's grasp. No one admitted to seeing who the killer was. Of course, there're some rumors going around, but that's really all they are."

She thanked him for the information.

"Come on, Toby," she said. "Breakfast awaits."

They left the hotel for the café. To her surprise, they found Lurvey there, calmly eating his way through a stack of flapjacks. He stood when she entered, and motioned for her and Toby to join him.

"When did you get back to town, Mr. Lurvey?" she asked.

"A little while ago. Didn't have a bit of luck. Wasted my time."

His nonchalance irritated her. She struggled to keep her voice pleasant. "I guess I'd better fill you in on what's been happening while you were wasting your time."

She'd given him pause. "Please do," he said.

"It appears that Bledsoe stationed himself across the street from the hotel last night and tried to kill Shad. Or Abe. Maybe both. Thankfully, he failed. While the marshal was taking him down to the jail, somebody killed him with one of those little two-shot lady's pistols."

She figured it was a good thing they were all seated, else Lurvey would have been shocked off his feet.

"Did anybody get a look at Bledsoe's killer?"

"No, apparently not. But the one most likely to be

toting a derringer around in her reticule is Inez Schultz. She's up to her neck in this. Anyway, Abe left a note for me. The hostler delivered it a little while ago. He and Shad are headed south on the trail of Todd and the rest of the gang."

"And you and the boy here are getting ready to high-tail it after him," Lurvey said, a wry expression on his face.

"We can't be more than eight or nine hours behind. We've got to go. If you care anything about your bosses' interests, you'll be riding along, too. It seems to me you've wasted enough time looking for leads that don't exist."

He met her gaze without wavering. "You have a sharp tongue, Miss Russell, but unfortunately you're right. You two have your breakfast and meet me at the livery stable. Say in half an hour?"

"Half an hour it is," she agreed.

When they got there, they found that Lurvey had rented a couple of horses since his own was in sore need of rest. He was ready to ride. He waited while Toby saddled and bridled Banjo and fetched the clay-bank that he'd escaped on. Lark got the strawberry saddle that Cornelius had loaned her. The blood bay was back on a lead line. When the three of them rode down the main street of Cimarron, Lark had an unsettling feeling that she was being watched. She glanced back in time to catch a glimpse of Inez Schultz ducking into the mercantile.

At the edge of town, they turned south. Beyond the outskirts stood a large house that set off by itself. The townspeople called it the Schultz Place.

"Fancy, isn't it?" said Lurvey as he stared at the imposing structure.

"I believe it suits Mrs. Schultz's taste," said Lark. "Like its owner, it's expensive and gaudy."

They rode on past. At first, they followed the tracks that Shad and Abe had left. But soon there were others to follow. All appeared to be going in the same direction.

"We're riding parallel to the Santa Fe Trail that's east of here," said Lurvey. "Although you probably know it better than I do."

"I'm a freighter, Mr. Lurvey. You'd know that if our paths had ever crossed at Last Chance."

"No, you wouldn't," said Toby. "Lark keeps herself disguised as a man. Bet she fools most everyone."

Lurvey looked at her with amusement. It was yet another thing about him that she resented.

"I'm guessing they're headed for Rayado," she said. "But I'd bet my last dollar they'll be going a whole lot farther than that."

She had no takers.

The ground contained a confusion of tracks. While Lark was no expert, she could tell that Shad and Abe were following five outlaws and a large number of mules.

When they came to the wash, she stared at the burned remains of the animals, thinking of her own team back at Last Chance.

"They brought replacements," said Lurvey. "There're tracks over there across the wash. Deep ones."

She looked to where he was pointing. "They'll certainly be easy to follow. We'd better get on with it."

They skirted the town of Rayado. A couple of miles beyond, the tracks led into the Santa Fe Trail.

"What a mess," Lark said, looking at the results of countless wagons of cargo, pulled by mules and oxen, as well as the effects of wind, rain, and mud.

"No sign of 'em up ahead, either," said Lurvey. "My guess is they turned off at some point."

"Where do you think they're going?" asked Toby.

"Somewhere to lay low, I expect. Probably the mountains. I can't think of a better place. Help me watch for any sign of where they've left the trail."

As it turned out, he didn't need their help. He was the one who spotted the turnoff.

"This way," he said.

Except for his occasional remarks that irritated her, Lark was finding that she liked Lurvey. This surprised her. But he was comfortable to be with. Toby seemed to like him too. This made their close association easier, especially when they camped for the night. Lurvey was always the gentleman. But her thoughts and concerns were with Abe. What was he doing? Was he all right? If something happened to him and Shad, would she be able to sense it? The closer she got to the *Sangres*, where Lurvey believed they were heading, the greater her sense of urgency. Two men against five. How in the world could they possible survive?

Chapter Thirteen

Shad slid from the saddle and tied the dun to a low-hanging tree limb. Then he hurriedly exchanged his boots for the soft leather moccasins in his saddlebag. This was a job that would require stealth. He made sure his gun was loaded and that he had plenty of ammunition. Now he was ready to make the climb. He proceeded slowly and carefully so as not to make any sound that would give him away. The way he figured it, there was only one outlaw up there watching the approaches to the cabin. Strong was discounted because of his wound. Someone else had been hit in the gunfight, too, but that again might have been Strong.

He wondered about Schultz. The barkeep appeared to be more of a prisoner than a gang member. Shad doubted if the others would trust Schultz to go off on his own. It was clear that Inez Schultz was the strong one in that family and that she commanded more respect from the outlaws than her husband. Most likely, it was Mohler, Thurman, or Todd up there. But if he'd read Todd right, he was the kind that always left the dirty work to others.

Keeping low, Shad moved quietly through the underbrush. From somewhere close by, a horse snorted. He froze. His enemy was close. He glanced down at the cabin, but from where he was crouched, it was hidden from view. That meant he was also hidden from anyone who might be watching from below. Dense pine needles screened him from the outlaw above. His wounded side throbbed with pain, but at least the bleeding had stopped. He licked his dry lips to moisten them. Just as he was about to move on, he heard a dislodged rock tumble downward with a rattle. There was yet another horse on the mountainside.

"Mohler, is that you?" called a voice that he recognized as belonging to Thurman.

"Shut up!" came the quick response. "He's around here, somewhere. I've been tracking him."

Shad was caught between the two outlaws. Both were determined to kill him and there was nowhere to turn. He decided to make the first move instead of waiting for them to find him. Mohler was the predator. He wouldn't expect an attack from his quarry. Holding his left arm close to protect his injured side, Shad gripped the pearl-handled .44 with his right hand.

"Are you sure you know what you're talking about?" said Thurman. "I ain't seen hide nor hair of him."

"Then why don't you shut up and look!"

They started to close in from both sides. He could hear them moving through the underbrush. Now was the time. He turned back toward Mohler, who was working his way uphill. It required only a few yards to bring them face-to-face. Not more than a dozen paces separated the two. Shad was partly hidden by branches and it took his enemy an extra second to spot him.

"Drop your gun, Mohler," he ordered.

"Why you . . ." he started.

"Yeah, it's me. I told you to drop your gun and get down off your horse. I won't tell you again."

Shad watched through squinted eyes as the big man hesitated. He knew exactly what thought must be going through the outlaw's mind. He braced himself. When Mohler went to grab iron, he was ready. He raised the .44 and shot him out of the saddle.

"Mohler!" shouted Thurman on hearing the gun shot. "Are you all right? Did you get him?"

There was nothing but silence as he waited for the answer that didn't come. Then Shad could hear Thurman moving through the underbrush again. He had to get moving himself. He needed to find cover.

"Wakefield!" yelled Thurman. "Don't try to hide. I know you're up here."

Shad turned to his right and followed the curve of the mountain. He was thankful for the moccasins that made no sound and left only the faintest tracks. Once he looked back to see if the outlaw was following. It was then that he stumbled and fell. Quickly he scrambled to his feet. His shirt was wet. The wound was bleeding again.

"That you, Wakefield?" came the taunting voice that was now much closer. "Just stay where you are, I'm coming for you."

Shad ran. At this high altitude, the air was thin. His lungs were laboring to take in enough to sustain him. Then he saw the large, dead-fall limb. It wasn't much in the way of cover, but it would have to do. His strength was failing him and Thurman was closing the distance between them.

He climbed over the log and crouched down, waiting for the inevitable. His left arm, held tight against his side, stanched the flow of blood. Seconds passed. Then he saw the outlaw approaching. Thurman had noticed the blood. He appeared cocky, as if he was certain he'd run Shad to ground like a wounded, helpless animal.

"Why don't you come on out, Wakefield," he called. "Make it easy on yourself."

Shad remained silent, feeling his pulse pounding in his ears.

He knew he was going to have to kill Thurman or be killed himself. It was plain that the outlaw was growing impatient. When his patience ran out, shots would be exchanged at close range. Shad knew he would have only one chance. He'd have to make it count.

He rose to one knee, pistol in hand.

"Are you looking for me, Thurman?" he said.

The red-headed outlaw's eyes widened in surprise. He also had his gun in his hand. Before he could squeeze the trigger, he noticed the pearl grips on Shad's weapon and recognized it as his own. That instant of hesitation gave Shad the edge. He fired. Thurman got off a shot, too, but it went wild, for Shad's bullet had already reached its target. Red Thurman fell. He'd never get up again.

For a minute or two Shad stayed behind the deadfall, letting his breathing and heartbeat get back to normal. He felt weak, but this was no time to give in. He had to get back to Squire. And there was still Todd to be reckoned with. Nor would it do to discount Strong or Schultz. Finally, after reloading the empty chambers in his gun, Shad struggled to stand. On unsteady feet he went over to make sure that Thurman was dead. Strange, he thought. In death, the man's face looked almost benign, something he'd never looked in life. He found the outlaw's horse where it had wandered off and pulled Thurman's rifle from its scabbard.

Down at the cabin, Todd would surely have heard the gunshots, although he'd be left to wonder about the outcome.

Squire was still tied to the limb where Shad had left him. He grabbed the dun's reins and climbed into the saddle. He was aware of the warm wetness on his shirt and glanced down. Blood from his side was clotting and there was only a slight seepage now. For that he was thankful.

Carefully, he made his way down the slope on horseback. Both of the outlaws' mounts were following Squire's lead. He paused at a spot where he could see below and not be seen. Schultz was out in front of the cabin. The barkeep was shielding his eyes, looking up toward the place where Thurman had been stationed. Not seeing anything, he went back inside and closed the door.

Shad headed down to the cabin, first making a detour so he could approach on its blind side. He'd reached the bottom of the slope when a flash of light caught his eye. Sunlight was reflecting on gunmetal. An outlaw was crouched just behind the corner of the hideout. Shad left the saddle at the same instant a shot was fired. Rolling as he hit the ground, he came up with the pistol in his hand. The outlaw fired again. A bullet plowed into the ground in the same spot where he'd been a second earlier.

He couldn't see the shooter's face, but he got a glimpse of a black shirt like the one Todd had worn in Last Chance. Shad was caught out in the open, giving Todd a clear shot from the cover of the cabin wall. There was nothing to do but make a run for it. He was up and sprinting toward the trees when the third and fourth shots rang out. They hit so close on his heels that the dirt they sprayed up stung his ankles above the moccasins. He counted another shot and reached the cover of the woods just as the sixth bullet slammed into a nearby tree, sending wood chips flying. One of them bit into his neck like a wasp. He slapped his hand against it.

With six shots spent, Todd would have to reload. This was Shad's one chance. But time was short.

Todd was around the front corner, his attention on reloading his pistol. Shad left the protection of the trees and ran to the blind-side wall of the hideout. As soon as Todd had finished, he fired off another shot at the tree. Shad inched his way to the edge of the cabin.

"Give it up, Wakefield!" called Todd. "If you come on in, I'll cut you in on a share of the gold!"

Shad was close now. Within a few steps. He crouched low and lunged past the corner, turning at the same time to thrust his pistol into the gut of the startled outlaw.

"Drop it, Todd!"

Having no choice, the outlaw tossed his gun aside and raised his hands.

"Now, let's go inside and have a word with the rest of your gang."

The look on Todd's face was one of pure hatred.

"What gang?" he asked. "Who's left? I take it you got Mohler and Thurman. You must have gotten

Quillen back on that mountain. Strong died from his wounds, both of them thanks to you. There's no one left but me and that half-witted barkeep."

"You in there," Shad called. "Come out here with your hands up."

Schultz appeared. He looked smaller than Shad remembered, and he had a sickly look on his face.

"Don't shoot," he pleaded. "I didn't want to be a part of this. It was Inez. She got me into this deal and they made me come along with them. They've worked me like a slave."

Todd gave a snort of disgust.

From what he'd seen, Shad believed the barkeep. He figured a jury would, too. Most likely they'd go easy on him. Todd was a different story. After the brutal murder of those four miners who were serving as guards, there was almost certain to be a hangman's noose in his future.

"Tie him up," he ordered Schultz. The barkeep hurried to comply.

Once the killer was securely bound, Shad went inside to search for Abe.

"Your friend is fine," Schultz assured him. "Todd hit him on the head, that's all."

The interior looked dark after the bright New Mexico sunshine. It took a minute for his eyes to adjust. When they did, he scanned the sparsely furnished room before spotting Abe. His friend was trussed up, lying against the back wall.

"About time you got here, Shadrach," he said, his voice much weaker than usual. "Cut me loose, for Pete's sake, and tell me what's been going on."

Shad gave the job to Schultz while he kept his gun

on Todd. He was aware that a man who's determined to escape a hanging is apt to try anything.

When Abe was free, he sat up and started rubbing the circulation back into his wrists and ankles. It was then that he noticed the blood on Shad's torn shirt.

"Are you all right, son?"

"I am now."

He was keeping watch on the nervous-acting barkeep, as well as Todd.

"Where's the gold?" he asked.

Schultz nodded toward a lean-to room that had been added to the side.

"It's in there," he said.

Abe retrieved his gun. "I'll have a look."

He pulled back the curtain that closed off the room and let out a low whistle.

"I take it that it's there," said Shad.

"Yep. In all its splendor. I'll watch 'em while you have a look."

What Shad saw as he stood in the curtained doorway was a treasure to dazzle the eye. It was the same stuff that had lured the Conquistadors northward. It had also driven men crazy with gold fever. It had even turned some of them into thieves and killers. But impressive as this stash of gold was, he doubted that it comprised the entire shipment. Turning back, he confronted Schultz.

"Where's the rest of it?"

The barkeep heaved a big sigh. "I guess I might as well tell you. It's buried in back of my carriage house."

"How can that be?" said Abe. "We already dug that up. There wasn't anything there but the remains of the wagon and one of the mules."

"Exactly. In case somebody got nosy and started

digging, that's what they wanted them to think. After finding the carcass and the wood, they were apt to stop. To find the gold, you have to go deeper. It was put in first and covered with a ground cloth. Then the other stuff was thrown in on top."

"Not a bad idea," said Abe. "I wonder who thought . . ."

He was interrupted by the sound of a horse approaching. Shad stepped over to the doorway and looked out.

"Well, well, Lurvey finally decided to join the party," he said.

The mine owners' agent reined up in front of the cabin and slid off his horse. Shad stepped outside.

"Glad to see you're still alive and kicking," said Lurvey. "Sorry I'm late."

"It turned out we didn't need you, after all. Todd and Schultz are inside. The rest of them are dead."

"Looks like I rode all this way for nothing."

"On the contrary," said Abe from inside the doorway. "You're just in time to help us pack the gold back to Cimarron."

Lurvey went inside and glanced at the subdued-looking Schultz. "Is it true that he and his wife were in on it?"

"Yep," said Abe, "but mostly it's his wife. I don't expect Mrs. Schultz will be needing her carriage house or fancy clothes for a long time to come."

"It serves her right," said Schultz. "I wish to heaven I'd never met her."

"And the others are dead, you say?"

"Yes. Strong died from his wounds. I had to kill Mohler and Thurman."

Lurvey nodded. "I understand. Been in that situation a time or two, myself. Right now, I've got a couple of friends who're waiting for my signal to ride in."

"You don't mean to say that Lark came with you?" said Abe, surprise registering on his face.

"I don't rightly know how I could have stopped her. Toby's with us, too."

When they got to the cabin, Lark insisted on cleaning and dressing Shad's wound. Then she raided the outlaws' supplies and prepared them a feast. At least it seemed like a feast to Shad, who'd had nothing to eat for a while.

When they were done, they went out and collected the bodies to be put underground. Then they took turns guarding Todd and Schultz through the night.

Come morning, they loaded the gold into packs and put the mules to work again. Shad helped a little before he was ordered to stop. Before leaving, they made sure the bonds on Todd were secure. Schultz was tied also. In spite of his demeanor, Shad didn't quite trust him. At last the strange procession made its way down from the mountains.

It was on the third day that Lurvey dropped back and rode beside Shad.

"You're looking a lot better than you did the other day," he said.

"Guess I'll do."

"I'm expecting the gentlemen Blair, Brownsworth, and Hale to be most grateful for this cargo we're returning."

"Along with the part that's buried at Cimarron?"

"That, too. You'll be getting a sizeable reward. How you split it is up to you."

He hadn't been thinking of a reward, but he and his friends had earned one, for sure.

"I expect I'll divide it even."

"However you want to do it is fine with me and the bosses."

Shad wished they could move along faster. The mine owners could wait. But Nat Granger couldn't.

Chapter Fourteen

Under the afternoon sun, they rode into Cimarron. There were seven of them with six loaded pack mules. Curious townspeople came out on the boardwalk to watch the peculiar entourage. Two of the riders were obviously prisoners. One was known to them.

Shad and the others reined up in front of the jail to deliver Todd and Schultz. Inside, Shad told his story to Marshal Glover, as well as to the wiry, hard-faced sheriff, who'd returned from his manhunt.

"Inez Schultz is into this up to her neck," he concluded. "Much more so than her husband, in my judgment."

"Well," said Glover, "we've got plenty of room for her here in the jail. By the way, two of them three mining moguls hit town awhile back. They've got themselves set up in rooms at the National Hotel. One of 'em is getting downright testy waiting for you to show up."

"Good," said Lurvey. "I sent word to them before I left town."

"Speak of the devil," said Glover, glancing out the window. "Here they come, now."

Rossman Blair walked into the jail like he owned it. Anyone watching would think he owned New Mexico. Though his mustache was sprinkled with gray, he had a trim build and a fine tailor. His jawline was sharply defined, and when he removed his hat, it was plain to see that his hair had been recently cut by a barber who knew his business. The slightly older Brownsworth was only a little less imposing.

"We've come to retrieve our cargo," Blair announced. "Of course, there will be a sizeable reward for its recovery."

"I expect we've earned it," said Shad. "But not all of the gold is out there on those mules."

Blair's expression hardened. "And where might it be?"

"Out behind the Schultz's carriage house."

"Then get it," said Blair.

"Get it yourself. I'm going over to the Doc's and get patched up."

Blair seemed to notice Shad's wound for the first time. "One moment," he said, fixing him with his gaze. "They said you only brought in two prisoners."

Shad was losing patience with the mogul's arrogance. "I brought in your man, Todd, along with the barkeep, Schultz. The rest are dead, except for Inez Schultz, who took part in this scheme and is running loose somewhere in Cimarron."

Blair's lips tightened into a slit and his face turned red. "Why, we had dinner with Mrs. Schultz last evening," said Brownsworth. "She was a charming woman. Extremely interested in this robbery and how the investigation was being handled. She had nothing good to say about the marshal, by the way, nor about any of you, for that matter."

"I wouldn't expect so," said Shad. "She was making a fool of you."

"Arrest that woman!" Blair bellowed. "Right now."

Glover glanced over at Shad and strapped on his gun. "I expect I'd better. If she saw you come into town, she's apt to make a run for it."

Shad decided to postpone his visit to the doctor and tag along instead. He wanted to be there when the woman was arrested and hauled to jail like the criminal she was.

When they got to her house, Inez Schultz was frantically climbing into her carriage, which was hitched to a pair of matched roans. It had been haphazardly loaded with her expensive clothes, jewelry, and a silver service.

"Don't forget, she carries a derringer," Shad warned.

While he watched, the marshal disarmed and arrested Inez. All the while she was threatening and protesting. But nothing she could say was going to do her any good.

"We'd better retrieve that gold," said Lurvey.

Out back, he and Toby set to work and dug up the animal carcass and wagon parts while the moguls looked on anxiously. Then Lurvey got to one knee and ripped up the ground cloth. There, fully exposed, was the gold that had lain beneath it. Standing there, staring at the shiny metal, Blair looked almost happy.

Shad took his leave then and went back to the hotel,

where he bathed and changed his clothes. When he was presentable, he rode over to the doctor's place to have him take a look at his wound.

"It's doing fine," said Dr. Tomlin when Shad had stripped to the waist. "You took care of it pretty well and avoided infection. There's not much more I can do for you except clean it and apply a fresh bandage."

"Good enough."

He paid the doctor when he'd finished, and went back to his room for a much-needed rest.

The following day turned out to be a busy one. Blair and his partners arranged for a substantial reward to be deposited in Shad's name at the Bank of Trinidad. Then Shad and the others got ready to ride. Not only were they taking Toby back to Colorado, they were bringing Lark along, as well. Abe had been talking to her of marriage, and she'd made the decision to leave her life as a teamster behind.

"It's been nice working with you," said Lurvey, shaking hands all around as he saw them off. "I'll take the hermit's horse back to him and hire the Kinion boy at Last Chance to take care of Miss Larkspur's mules."

"We'd be obliged," said Abe.

Without a backward glance, they rode out of the trail town and headed north.

The four of them pressed on, putting the miles behind them. They arrived at the ranch in time for Toby to make peace with his father. In fact, they had three whole days together before Nat passed away quietly in his sleep. When Shad saw the two of them together, he felt that the journey he'd made had been worth it, in spite of all the difficulties. Toby seemed to mature overnight. He decided on his own to stay on at the M Bar W and work as a ranch hand.

"I've had enough adventure in the last few weeks to last me for a long, long time," he said. "Besides, this is where Pa wanted me to be."

It wasn't long after the Judge had presided over Nat's burying that he began to think about presiding over a wedding.

It was a couple of weeks after their return to Colorado that Lark and Abe were married in the big front room of Shad's ranch. For the happy occasion, it was decked out in bright yellow-leaf cottonwood branches.

After the promises were made, the couple hitched, and the food consumed, the newlyweds set out for Abe's place in Trinidad. When the house was empty of guests, Shad and the Judge sat back in the big leather chairs near the fireplace and drank a toast.

"To home," said Judge Harley Madison, lifting his glass.

"To home," said Shad.

He was truly glad to be here.